I'M FOLLOWING YOU

EMILY SHINER

INKUBATOR
BOOKS

Published by Inkubator Books
www.inkubatorbooks.com

Copyright © 2022 by Emily Shiner

Emily Shiner has asserted her right to be identified as the author of this work.

ISBN (eBook): 978-1-83756-051-6
ISBN (Paperback): 978-1-83756-052-3
ISBN (Hardback): 978-1-83756-053-0

1

COLLETTE

"**B**aby sister, you know I love you, but you can't stay here tonight." I drunkenly whisper the words into Arabella's hair, pulling her closer to me so I can really breathe her in. "You need to hurry home to Henry. What would he do without you?"

"He'd find somewhere else to sleep." She giggles, hugging me back. "Besides, weren't you telling me I need to put myself out there more often? Live a little? Meet people?"

"Yes." Pushing her back so I can really look at her, I pause while I gather my thoughts. It's hard. They're slippery with all the gin I've had tonight. "But I meant out with friends, at a bar. Or something. Not at my house. Think of how much fun you could be having on a Friday night instead of hanging out here watching me drink."

"See, that's the problem." She wriggles out of my grasp and grabs her purse, throwing it on her shoulder. "I don't drink, so what would I do at a bar with a lot of drunken people? They're annoying."

I shoot her a look. She returns it.

"You might meet someone who got roped into being the

EMILY SHINER

designated driver for his friends," I point out. "Or her friends. Either way, I really don't care."

Now she laughs and pulls me in for another hug. "I love you, Collette, but I'm not going to even consider meeting someone at a bar. Besides, I have Henry."

"Henry is an eight-year-old cat who vomits in my shoes when I come to visit you."

"Yes, but he's *my* eight-year-old cat, and he loves me. I'm happy, Collette, okay? You don't have to worry about me."

But I do. I worry about Arabella, always have, probably always will. It's not that I feel like she needs to be married or be in a serious relationship to be happy, but maybe I wouldn't worry about her so much. I'm not in a relationship, but I'm older. She's always needed someone to take care of her, and that's always been me.

And I've been happy to do it, but what if I weren't here for her?

"I do worry about you," I tell her, watching her pull her keys from her purse. "I worry about you because I love you. If you want to spend the night here, you can, okay?" I offer what I know she wants even though I don't really want her to stay.

I love my sister, and I'll do anything to protect her, but after she leaves, I have someone else coming over. The last thing I want is for Arabella to find out that I'm encouraging her to jump into a serious relationship while I'm sleeping with a guy down the hall who thinks that McDonald's is fine dining and always signs off his texts with *be cool*.

"No, no, I need to head home to the old curmudgeon. You need water before I go? Tylenol? Someone to hold your hair back while you puke?"

"I'm not going to puke."

"That's good. I'll check on you in the morning, okay? Love you."

"Love you." I'm antsy for her to leave now, but I don't want her to know that. Plastering a smile on my face, I walk her to the door, glancing out into the hall to make sure he's not headed this way yet. I can't smell the cloud of pot that always accompanies him, so I'm good.

Arabella throws me a wave before she reaches the stairs.

I grin back, relieved that she's out of here before she encounters Mike but also relieved that she seems okay. My younger sister is the most important thing to me.

Forty minutes later I've picked up the snacks we were eating while watching a movie and swept the floor. Mike should be here by now and I'm honestly a little annoyed I kicked Arabella out and he hasn't shown up. Even though it won't make him get here any faster, I keep checking my phone, wondering where he is. But I refuse to call him. Mike tends to do things on his own time, which is just one of the reasons why this isn't ever going to be a long-term thing with him. I'm in the middle of refreshing my drink again when there's a loud knock on the door.

Finally.

"You know you don't have to knock," I call, taking a sip of my drink. "I know you're coming, so you can let yourself in."

He knocks again.

"Come on, man," I mutter, putting my drink down on the coffee table. I'm about to leave it when I remember Arabella telling me that I need to start using a coaster so I don't ruin my furniture. It takes a moment to find one and slip it under my drink, but the knock comes again.

"Listen, if you're so eager, you can come in." Throwing the door open, I pop one hip out to the side. My shirt has slipped down over one shoulder, a look I'm sure will drive him nuts. He's a lot of fun, but he's definitely not Mr. Right, not by a long shot.

He is, as they say, Mr. Right Now, but only when my sister

doesn't know and only when it's in the privacy of my own apartment so nobody will know either.

But it's not Mike.

"Collette Jones?" The mountain of a man standing in front of me is wearing a uniform, his badge somehow shining even in the gloom of the hallway. He's frowning. His partner, standing next to him and a bit behind, has a strange expression on his face.

Is it concern?

The second man shifts his feet.

"I'm Collette," I say, finally finding my voice. "Is there a problem?"

"Do you know Arabella Jones?"

No. God, no, this can't be happening.

All the gin I had earlier this morning threatens to come back up. I swallow hard, reaching out and grabbing the doorframe for support. When I open my mouth to answer him, no sound comes out.

So I nod.

"Mrs. Jones, your sister was in an accident a few blocks away."

No. Dear God, I'll do anything. I'll change however you want, I'll donate money and time, and I'll be a better friend. I'll be a better listener. I won't get mad at people when they jaywalk. I won't —

"Do you understand what I've said, Mrs. Jones?"

"Ms.," I correct him, unable to wrap my mind around what he said.

"Ms. Jones, do you understand what I said? Do you have anyone you can call?"

A shiver tears through me, and I slowly sink to the floor. The man doesn't move, but his partner kneels next to me. "Ms. Jones, who can we call? Is there anyone we can reach out to for you so you don't have to be alone?"

I can't answer him. I know I should, that they expect me to respond to them.

I can't.

"Is she..." My voice trails off.

I can't say it.

"Ms. Jones." The officer kneeling next to me sighs, then looks up at his partner before focusing his attention on me again. "You need to understand that she didn't suffer. It was instant; it was..."

But I'm already tuning him out. It doesn't matter if she didn't suffer. It doesn't matter what happened. My baby sister, the best person in the world, is dead.

And it's all my fault.

COLLETTE

The thing about grief is that it can be so overwhelming that it threatens to pull you down and drown you. I'm drowning now, or that's what my therapist tells me, and that's why I'm here.

Group grief counseling.

I shift in my seat, trying to keep the blood flowing to my legs. These chairs are uncomfortable. I can't help but think that someone came along and cut half an inch off of one leg of each chair to make it so you have to remain perfectly rigid when sitting in them.

It's like that way cops torture people when they interrogate them. The lights are too hot, the chairs are uneven, and when you drink the coffee, they fingerprint the cup.

My eyes flick over to the coffee and donuts on the table at the side of the room. They're there for us to eat after the counseling, after all of us have had time to spill our guts about how messed up we are.

A woman sits down next to me, casting me a shy smile as she does. "Hi, I'm Linda." She already has a cup of coffee in her hand and glances down at it when she sees me stare at it. "I need my caffeine to make it through these meetings. Is this your first one?"

I nod. Stiff. Everything about this place is miserable, but it's where Carol, my therapist, told me I need to come.

It'll help you improve. You'll do better in a group setting where you can see that your grief isn't going to kill you. You're not alone, Collette. You need to understand that.

Looking around the room, though, I can't help but think that grief is slowly killing everyone in here. Even the man sitting in the chair in the middle of the semicircle looks like he's been put through the wringer. His shirt is wrinkled and untucked; the laces on one of his loafers have come untied.

"Well, you're going to love Vince," Linda tells me, leaning over like we're schoolgirls in the cafeteria discussing our latest crushes. "He really is amazing, and he makes you feel so much better about what happened. Trust me, you'll love talking to him."

I highly doubt it.

The only thing that would make this better is putting my arms around Arabella again. Barring that, I wouldn't mind...

Nope. Not going to go there. Do I think group grief counseling is a crock? Yes, I do.

But I'm still going to give it a shot, if only because every morning feels like I'm waking up under the ground and clawing my way through the dirt. By the time I go to bed, I'm in the open air, gasping, my lungs filled with dirt, but in the morning I'm back in the ground.

Just like Arabella is.

Shaking my head, I push that thought from my mind.

Vince clears his throat, and all chatter around the circle stops.

I'm relieved, not because I want to share how I feel in this group, but because the sooner we start, the sooner this will all be over.

"Welcome, everyone. I hope you're all having a wonderful evening." Vince leans forward on his chair. Behind him I can see rain pounding into the window. "It's definitely nicer in here than it is out there."

A few chuckles.

I don't laugh.

"Why don't we start? I know everyone has their eyes on the coffee and donuts. As you all know, I'm Vince."

"Hello, Vince." Everyone speaks at once.

I jump.

Creepy. Just like they always show it on TV, like this is a cult or something.

"I'm here to lead this group, but that doesn't mean I don't know what you're going through. As your leader, I'm here to guide the group and offer support, but I'm no better than anyone else in this circle." He pauses, looking around, making sure to lock eyes with everyone.

I shift, my chair squeaking in response. Instead of meeting his gaze, I look right between his eyebrows.

"And I'm really excited that we have someone new here tonight. Collette, is it? Why don't you go ahead and introduce yourself to the group so we can all get to know you."

I freeze. Everyone turns to look at me.

"Um." When I clear my throat, the sound is loud. "Hi. I'm Collette."

"Hello, Collette."

Their voices make me shiver.

"I'm here because my therapist told me I need to be here." I crack a smile.

Nobody returns it. They all look so serious.

"Thanks for having me."

"Collette, we're so glad that you're here. Do you care to tell us why your therapist wanted you to come?"

Do I? No, I don't, but I'm not sure if I have a choice.

"I lost my sister. She was killed by a drunk driver."

And I'm the reason she's dead. If I'd allowed her to stay with me the way she wanted to, if I'd not pushed her out the door, if I'd put her before the pothead down the hall, then she'd still be here, but I highly doubt anyone here wants to hear about that.

"Oh, Collette, I know that's hard. Thank you for being so open and vulnerable with us."

I nod, and he turns away. Relief floods through me.

And the driver who killed her is walking around free. Nobody seems to care that she put my Arabella in the ground. Nobody cares that she's still alive when my sister is dead. Nobody cares, and I can't seem to make anyone understand why this is so important to me.

Vince starts talking again. I promised my therapist that I'd not only listen to what was said here, but that I'd do my best to internalize it, but it's really hard. His voice fades away, feeling more like the background noise when you leave the TV on during dinner than anything else.

I should focus, but instead I look around the circle.

Everyone here has lost someone. That's what my therapist said, like knowing that would make me feel happier about coming here. But the last thing I want is to be surrounded by this much grief.

"I think it's all a load of shit," I hear someone whisper.

My head snaps around so I can see who was talking. It's a woman, older than me, with a cane clutched in her hand, whispering to the man next to her. He nods like he's listening, but his eyes are locked on me.

I risk a glance at his name tag. *Gavin.*

Shivering, I turn my attention back to Vince.

I know my therapist thinks coming here will be helpful for me, but I don't see how.

Surrounding yourself with more grief doesn't help you float.

It drags you under.

3

COLLETTE

A week later I'm back in group. Vince speaks, and I know I should listen to him, but instead I look down at a newspaper clipping. I'm gripping it so tightly that my hand shakes.

I've memorized the words, but I still look at it every night when I go to bed.

January 25

Courtney Barrow, 41, was found unresponsive in her parents' home last night. Barrow came to public attention because of her upcoming trial where she would face charges for the death of Arabella Jones. Barrow, after allegedly spending the evening drinking, hit Jones when she was leaving her sister's apartment, killing her instantly. With her court date approaching, police believe Barrow was unable to live with her grief and guilt over the death of Arabella Jones.

Folding the piece of newspaper, I tuck it back into my

purse, giving the pocket a gentle pat after I do. My therapist was surprised when I told her I carry it around with me everywhere, but it makes me feel better.

Think of it as a grown-up blankie.

Courtney's dead. All of the nightmares I've been having about her being alive aren't real. I need to remember that. Still, last night I woke up, drenched in sweat. I saw her face as she got in her car, saw her press down hard on the gas.

Saw her drive straight towards Arabella.

"Collette, are you with us today?" Vince's voice cuts through my thoughts.

"Yes." My fingers twitch to pull the newspaper clipping back out, but I stop myself. "Yes, I'm here. Sorry. I had a bad dream last night, and it got into my head."

He smiles. Next to me, Linda reaches out and lightly pats my knee. Nobody else moves.

"I dreamed that the woman who killed my sister was still alive. I know it's irrational to think that, because the police found her body, but I can't help it. It feels like she's still alive." I spread my hands out on my thighs and exhale hard. "It's not fair that she might be alive when Arabella isn't." The words pour out of me, and for a moment, it feels good to be open with the group.

The response is silence. Last week when I came to group, that concerned me, how everyone would fall silent when someone said something that made everyone stop and think. Now, though, I've heard enough of these long silences, even though it's only my second time here.

Nobody's judging me. At least, I don't think so. They're all thinking, as we try to figure out what to do and how to survive this.

"Intrusive thoughts aren't only about hurting ourselves." It's a new man speaking, someone I don't really know. I turn in surprise, having expected Vince to be the one to respond, then frown when I realize it's the same man who was staring at me last week. "Sometimes they're bigger than that. And they're normal. Everyone has intrusive thoughts, but that doesn't make them real. It makes them common. That doesn't mean you have to let them rule your life."

I swallow, nodding.

"Thanks, Gavin," Vince says. "I think you're right. I think we want to give weight to every single thought we have even though there's often no reason to. That's something you have to learn how to deal with, Collette. The more joy you add to your life, the less often you'll have these thoughts."

I want to argue and tell them that they weren't thoughts I was having. They were dreams, all in my head like someone screaming at me. Thoughts are something I can control. These I can't.

But what if she really isn't dead? What if Courtney is alive?

That thought is like a maggot, eating its way into my brain, making it impossible for me to think straight. I can't wrap my mind around that thought, but I can't push it away, either.

The rest of group flies by. Hearing other people's sad stories doesn't make me feel better about losing Arabella. This is supposed to make me not feel all alone; it's supposed to give me healthy coping skills.

But is it?

I don't really want to stick around for refreshments this evening, but I'm really hungry after working a bit longer than normal at the library. Being around all the books in the quiet of the library is calming to me, and I was happy to go in early this morning to help cover a co-worker's shift. Being there helps keep any thoughts of Arabella and Courtney out of my mind.

But as soon as I leave the sanctuary of the library, they come back in full force.

Holding a donut in my mouth so I can pour myself some coffee, I inch along the table, my eyes on another donut at the end. Surely nobody will care if I take more than one, right? I'm nibbling slowly, taking my time, ignoring the chatter around me, when something someone is saying makes me stop and listen.

"I'm only saying, Gavin, that sometimes intrusive thoughts are real. Sometimes our subconscious is trying to tell us things that we want to allow ourselves to believe."

Gavin's response is muffled.

Leaving the chocolate donut behind, I step back from the table, doing my best to look casual as I walk closer to the two men.

Gavin's facing me, his mouth a tight line. I know men like him, men who hate being told what to do. They hate being questioned when they've already stated something as fact. I'm glad I'm not the one standing up to him right now.

But this guy talking to him is voicing exactly what I was thinking earlier.

"Your subconscious has no role in this, Jackson. You have to be willing to separate yourself from your grief. Trust me, if you're told one thing and your subconscious tells you another, you need to believe what you're told." Gavin's face is red now, and he's gripping his coffee so hard that the Styrofoam sides are starting to bend in.

"That's where you and I can agree to disagree, Gavin." Jackson's voice is light. He doesn't seem at all stressed out by the conversation the two of them are having — not like Gavin is, anyway. "But I'll see you next week. I need to head home before it's too late."

He turns to leave, and I down my coffee, wincing as the hot brew burns my throat. Before I can lose my nerve, I force my feet to chase after him, pausing at the door only long enough to toss my cup in the trash. The donut follows.

"Excuse me?" We're outside now, and my voice barely carries through the thick air. It's going to rain again tonight, and the humidity is oppressive. "Jackson?"

The man stops and turns, running his hand through his hair as he does. He didn't sound particularly stressed when talking to Gavin, but I see it now, the tight look around his eyes, how his mouth is firm and his jaw is clenched.

"Hey, sorry to stop you when you were in a hurry," I say, the words falling out in a rush as I do my best to make him see that I need to talk to him. "But I heard what you were saying to Gavin." He cocks an eyebrow, and I speak faster. "I'm sorry, I wasn't trying to eavesdrop; it was just that you were saying what I was thinking the entire time he was talking during group."

"Oh." Now his face relaxes. He's surprised. "Oh, I didn't think anyone would really agree with me."

I know that I should have spoken up against Gavin, but I'd much rather live in my own mind. It's one of my worst traits, especially since losing Arabella.

"Yeah, I didn't speak up, I'm sorry." My face flames. "I just..."

"You're new." Jackson smiles at me, then glances down at my empty hands. "No coffee or donuts for you?"

I shake my head. Right now the coffee and few bites of donut I had are sitting heavy in my stomach, but I'm not going to admit that to this man. "I wanted to get out of there. Clear my head."

A stiff breeze blows across the parking lot, bringing with it the smell of the diner down the street. My stomach rumbles before I have a chance to realize that I'm even hungry.

"Great, come with me and let me buy you some food. It's the least I could do after you chased me down to tell me that I'm not crazy."

I hesitate. The last time I had anything close to a date

planned was the night I lost Arabella. Of course, it wasn't like Mike was anything resembling a real gentleman, and I'd never want to admit to anyone that it was a date with him, but it still feels strange to agree to grab something to eat with Jackson when I barely know him.

I hear my sister's voice in my head as clear as if she were standing next to me, talking right in my ear. *Go with him. Don't go back to the house to drown in your guilt on yet another evening.*

Still, even with those words bouncing around in my head, the next thing that comes out of my mouth surprises me.

"Yeah, that sounds great. Thanks. But I'm paying for myself."

"Perfect." He turns, obviously expecting me to follow him.

I do, if only because I'm curious and if only because I need to spend more time talking with someone else who understands how I feel.

4

COLLETTE

The diner is surprisingly busy when Jackson and I walk in. He gallantly holds the door for me, and I tip my head forward, letting my hair fall down by my face as I thank him. It *feels* like a date, but it's not.

It's two people who are both drowning, clinging to each other for a brief moment as we look for our footing.

"Just the two of you?" The server who appears in front of us is a teenager, with long black hair braided down her back and mint gum so strong I can smell it as she pops it at me. I nod, and she turns on her heel, more efficient than I've been in a while, leading us through the full tables.

We snag a table at the back of the diner, and I take the side of the table where I can keep my back to the wall. I've never liked being in a room where I can't see the door, and now I like it even less. It's smarter for me to be able to see what's coming, that way I can keep a look out for her. *Courtney.*

I'm beginning to think she's not just in my dreams.

The menus are large laminated trifolds that we have to balance on the table to see everything. In the end, Jackson orders a burger, and I order chicken fingers. They were my favorite food when I was younger and still make me happy when I eat them.

"So," Jackson says as I take a sip of my sweet tea, "tell me what you're really like. Outside of group."

Oh God.

I force myself to take a deep breath, both of my hands gripping the large cup my tea was served in. I feel the condensation on my skin, how cold it is, feel the sticky of the table's surface against my forearms.

He smiles. "I'm sorry, that came off strong, didn't it? I mean...we all put up walls when we're in group, don't we?"

"Yes." I feel myself relaxing. This guy isn't so bad. I need to let him in a touch. It's not a date. We're two people out to grab a bite to eat after grief group.

"I lost my wife to cancer," he tells me, and I freeze. Jackson always manages to be quiet during group, somehow deflecting really personal questions, while I can't seem to manage to do that. "It's been three years next month, but I swear it feels like yesterday. How long ago did you lose your sister?"

I have to force myself to put my glass down on the table before I can speak. My brain seems only to be able to do one thing at a time. "Um, about six months."

Five months, nineteen days, and twenty-two hours.

"Everyone tells you that it'll become easier," he says, giving me a nod. "And it does, but it takes a long damn time, so don't go looking for your life to suddenly become better."

"I'm not." I remember the dreams I've been having and how nice he was about them, how he didn't make me feel insane. At the same time, when I close my eyes, I can picture exactly what the newspaper clipping about Courtney says.

It doesn't make sense to me.

"Do you really think our subconscious could try to tell us

things even though we're not really ready to listen to it?" As soon as the words are out of my mouth, I clap my hand over my lips, trying to keep anything else from spilling out.

He pauses, then leans back as our waitress puts our food in front of us.

To avoid looking at him while he thinks about how to answer my question, I grab a hot fry and pop it in my mouth. It burns, but that feels good.

"You overheard what I was saying to Gavin, and I think yeah, it does. Scientists and doctors have studied our brains for years, trying to figure out exactly what they're capable of, and they keep being surprised. The more they learn, the more they realize they don't know anything." He takes a bite of his burger and gives me a one-shoulder shrug.

For a moment I don't answer. I roll his words around in my mind as I think about how they make me feel. That's another thing my therapist told me to do. Instead of speaking or acting, I'm supposed to take time to really consider how things make me feel and how I can respond to them.

We sit in silence for a moment before I finally figure out what to say. "The problem is that I feel out of touch with it all when I let myself go down this path. People keep telling me the drunk driver is dead, but I don't know that she is."

"Have you seen her?"

His question is so honest and makes so much sense that it actually catches me off guard for a moment. I close my eyes, picturing for a moment all of the women I walk by on a daily basis. Some of them, like tonight's waitress, are so obviously not the drunk driver that it's laughable. But have I seen her outside my dreams? Even when I'm sleeping, her face is distorted like I can't quite make out all of her features.

"Not yet," I admit, even though it feels terrible to do so. "I guess I haven't really been looking, though."

He nods. We fall silent again. I feel like I'm in therapy,

my mind racing as I try to figure out what I'm supposed to say next to make the person sitting across from me think I'm not crazy. Then again, Jackson doesn't. He made that clear when he was talking with Gavin about intrusive thoughts.

"Have you told anyone else in group about this? About thinking that she's still alive?"

I shake my head, feeling foolish. "I haven't besides what I said tonight. I...well, it hasn't come up. I don't know how to explain it to someone. Carol, my therapist, has told me over and over that she's dead. But I don't think she is."

"Please be careful." His words are measured. Careful. "I don't want anyone to think that you're not thinking things through clearly."

He can strive to hide what he really wants to say all he wants, but I know what it is. "You don't want people to think I'm crazy." I don't like how bitter I sound. "Do *you* think I'm crazy?"

"Not at all." He's looking at me, his eyes locked on mine, but unlike when Vince looks at me in group, this doesn't make me feel uncomfortable. "I have no reason to think you're crazy. I want you to make sure you aren't pegged as something you're not."

We eat in silence for a moment.

When he speaks again, his tone has changed, from low and worried to higher and unconcerned. "You know what? I have a plan. Do you work Saturday?"

His question surprises me, and I shake my head.

"Great, neither do I. Let's meet up downtown, walk around outside, enjoy some fresh air."

I interrupt him while he takes a breath. "We could look for her. The woman who killed Arabella." As soon as I speak, I wish I could take the words back. It's one thing for him to sit here with me and tell me he doesn't think I'm crazy, another entirely for him to want to go with me while I look for the woman who killed my sister.

But instead of telling me I've lost the plot or leaving, he nods.

"We'll see if we can find the drunk driver, okay? The weather is supposed to be beautiful, and I can't imagine anyone wanting to stay locked up in their house. If we find her, we find her. If we don't, then at least you'll have your answer, and you can —"

I hold my breath, praying that he isn't going to say *move on.*

"Feel like you did your best to find out the truth."

Thank God.

"Don't you have weekend plans?" It feels strange to rely on this man to help me through what I'm facing. Still, I like the thought of having his support. I like the thought of not being alone as I stumble my way through this. Carol doesn't want to even entertain the idea that the drunk driver is still alive.

But she is. Right? Why else would I keep dreaming about her? Why else would I feel so strongly about it?

The more I think about it, the more I allow my brain to entertain the thought, the more I know it to be true. Sitting here with Jackson, with his concern for me obvious, I'm confident that my mind has been trying to tell me that Courtney is still alive.

It's time that I listen. Especially now, especially with someone who wants to help me through this.

"Weekend plans? Not really. Without my wife..." His voice trails off; then he clears his throat. "Listen, Collette, I want to put all my cards on the table so there aren't any surprises later, okay? I want to help you on Saturday, but —"

"It's not a date." I finish the sentence for him as quickly as possible. "Not a date, we're two grief group friends walking around downtown. We don't even have to stop for lunch. In fact, we shouldn't."

A mixture of relief and happiness washes over his face. It shouldn't, but it takes me aback. When was the last time I made someone look that happy? My mind instantly returns to that night with Arabella, and I have to push away the thought.

She's gone, but the woman who killed her isn't, I know it.

And I'm going to find her.

5

AMANDA

I take a sip of wine to calm my nerves before slowly spinning in front of my bedroom mirror. My skirt twirls out from my body, but my top is nice and fitted. Isn't that what all the fashion gurus say to do? Fitted on top and loose on bottom or vice versa, but not tight all the way down?

Something like that.

"How do I look?" I ask the question even though there isn't anyone in my house to respond and then twirl one more time before grabbing my wine and draining the glass. It probably isn't the best idea to drink before I go out to lunch on a first date, but I can't help myself. I need something to control my nerves.

Putting the wineglass in the sink, I run some water in it, then grab my purse and head out the door. It's a gorgeous day, the first really nice Saturday that I've had off in a while. It feels like the past dozen of them have all been rainy and cloudy, and I've been itching to leave the house. My yard crew will be here later today, so when I return back from my date with Joe, everything should be cleaned up and taken care of.

It's a quick drive downtown, and I blast my music as I pull

up on Main Street, luckily snagging the last parking spot right in front of the restaurant. Tito's Tapas is my favorite place to eat. I love coming here every Saturday when I'm off to grab a bite to eat. Normally I'm by myself, but this is my comfort food, so I agreed to meet Joe here.

Hopefully I won't regret sharing this space with him. I couldn't come up with anywhere else I wanted to eat.

Besides, I've made so many decisions at work this week that I'm experiencing decision fatigue. Deciding what outfit to wear today and then to have red wine over white has used up all the brain power I have to make any decisions for the rest of the day. I'm not normally the type of person to let someone else order for me, but I might do that today.

We'll have to see how cute Joe really is. Beth, our mutual friend, told me he's not only cute, but tall, which is why I wore really high heels today. I can't wait to meet him, can't wait to have someone paying attention to me and smiling at me while I talk to them instead of crying through whatever I have to say.

But that's on me. I chose my job as an oncologist, and while I really do love it, there are always some times where there isn't anything I can do for the patient, and those are the cases that stick with me.

It seems like everyone in town is downtown today, and I have to push through a small crowd of people to go stand in front of the restaurant. Joe told me he'd be wearing jeans and a polo and would bring a flower, and I had texted back that I'd be on the lookout for him. It honestly feels like I'm the star in a romcom or something.

I mean, come on. He's bringing a flower to join me for our first date. Maybe we'll fall in love and be able to tell our kids how clichéd it was, but also how perfect. I'm excited, and I crane my neck this way and that as I look for him.

And then, he's here. Now, I'm not a gushy woman by any

means, but when he hands me the rose and then holds the door open for me, I feel my heart jump in my chest. Finally, someone who sees me for more than my white coat. This is going to be the start of something incredible, I know it.

It's going to be perfect. We'll sit by the window so we can watch everyone as they walk by, and I can't help but think that I'm not just getting to watch them. No, they have front-row seats to the start of something new. They get to see what a wonderful day I'm going to have.

They're all going to enjoy a first-row view to the best first date in the history of the world.

6

COLLETTE

"This is not a date. This is not a date. This is not a date."

Henry tilts his head and stares at me, his yellow eyes unblinking, the tip of his tail twitching from side to side. He's lived with me since we both lost Arabella, and while he still throws up in my shoes from time to time, I like to think the two of us have agreed on an uneasy truce.

"I'm serious, Hen, it's not a date. It's a mission. I can handle missions; I can't handle dates." Staring at myself in the mirror, I groan, then strip off the top I have on before replacing it with something much dumpier. The last thing I want is to give Jackson any idea that I might be interested in dating him. He *said* it wasn't a date, but I know how men can be.

They say one thing and mean another. But not this time, because there's no way he could possibly take one look at me and think that I'm trying to woo him. My shirt is a faux turtle-neck, sleeveless, so I don't die in this heat, but there's nothing sexy about that. My jeans aren't low rise or fitted or anything like that. I think they're called boyfriend jeans? Arabella swore by this style, but she made them look cute.

I make them look like I should be selling Bibles door-to-door with a long line of my children standing behind me, staring as I do.

"Perfect," I say, pulling my hair back into a ponytail and slipping some sunglasses on the top of my head. I made sure to eat a big breakfast and a hearty snack so I wouldn't be tempted to ask Jackson to stop and grab something to eat with me. This is a reconnaissance mission.

In the spirit of it being not-a-date, I told him I'd meet him downtown instead of giving him my address to pick me up. Pulling into the free parking lot two blocks off Main Street, I glance at my watch and then pick up the pace. I'm going to be a few minutes late, but that should be okay. It will show him how much of not-a-date this really is.

By the time I reach Main Street, he's there, leaning casually against a tree behind a couple sharing an ice-cream cone on a bench. He sees me and smiles, and I do a little check.

Nope, no butterflies. This is serious.

"Thanks for waiting for me," I say, but he waves off what else I was going to say.

"I think you're right on time. Main Street is packed. Now, tell me everything about this person so I can help you see if she's here."

I feel a flush of excitement. He really wants to help me. Whether or not he actually believes that Courtney is still alive isn't something I'm going to worry about right now. I'm going to play this cool and see what we can find. Besides work at the library, this is easily the largest crowd of people I've been around since Arabella's funeral.

It makes me grateful to have someone here to help me handle the crowd.

"Okay." I clear my throat. "Her name is Courtney Barrow.

She's older than me; I think she's forty-one." I *know* she's forty-one, but I don't want to seem like I've memorized all of her personal information. "Really pretty. Confident. Drinks too much. Obviously."

"Good. Then let's check out some of the local watering holes. Even if she's not in a bar, she might be someplace that sells a lot of alcohol. What do you think?"

"I think this is great." I rub my hands together. Even though the sun is out today, I feel cold. "Seriously, this is great. Okay. Let's start walking."

We do, trying to join in the flow of the people walking up the sidewalk. From time to time we stop, casually looking in the windows of each restaurant. I feel myself growing frustrated when we've gone three blocks, but I also know I don't want to give up.

"You okay?" Jackson stops, grabbing me by the elbow for a moment before letting me go.

I turn to him and take a deep breath. "Do you really think this is going to work?"

"Finding her?"

I nod.

"Do you think she's alive?"

I nod again. He's not looking at me like I'm crazy. He's looking at me like he really wants to help me.

"Then I think we need to try, okay? Tell me what she looks like. Her hair, her face. Is she short or tall? Skinny?"

"She's pretty. Blonde, but she could change her hair." My voice is flat. Monotone. "Don't you think she could change her hair?"

"You're right. How about this, then — we'll keep looking. We're almost finished with this side of Main Street, and then we'll come back on the other side. Then, if we don't see her —"

"She's really dead."

"Or we missed her. I want to help you, Collette. It's obvious you need to do this — need to look for her — to force her out of your head. There's absolutely no reason why you should have to do that on your own, okay? This is obviously a big deal to you, and there's no reason for you to go through it on your own. Other people may not understand, but I want to help you through this. If she's alive, we'll find her."

"Thank you." The words stick in my mouth. Yes, I have a therapist. And yes, I have a grief group. But this feels really good, like he cares about me and is willing to get out of his comfort zone to help me. I can't say I don't appreciate it.

"Don't mention it. I'd want someone to do the same for me. This is what will happen. I'll point some people out if they seem like the right age, okay? And if they're sitting in there drinking, then that's even better. You tell me if you think you see her."

The crowd moves around us. I'd forgotten there's a popular antique show downtown this weekend, which explains the influx of people. Had I remembered, I might have chosen to stay home, but then again, chances are good she came here to walk around and grab a drink before doing some shopping.

This is my best shot, and I don't have to do it alone.

I nod, and we step back into the flow of foot traffic, making our way past a jewelry store, a bank, and a thrift store. I don't even turn my head to look in the windows here because I already know Courtney won't be in there. Jackson is right — if we're going to find her downtown, then she's going to be somewhere she can drink.

The next block is mostly filled by a habitat resale store, and I keep my eyes firmly away from the sofas and knick-knacks in the window as I scan the faces of the people walking past us. Every once in a while I think I see her. A woman will have the same severe nose, the same full lips.

I think for a moment she's coming towards us, and I stop walking. Someone jostles me forward, and Jackson turns, his face full of concern.

I shake my head. *Not her.*

Then it happens. We reach the windows of Tito's Tapas, a bougie place with a tacky name. I've been lured in once before, thinking I could afford to eat there, but there wasn't any way. It's super expensive, and it has a whole row of seats at the window where patrons can sit and feel superior to everyone walking by.

"Nobody in here?" Jackson gestures at the window with his head. "There's that one woman, on the end. Look at her, with her wine. You said she was a bit older than you are, and that she's pretty. This woman is drinking, too. She's —"

But I don't hear what else he's going to say because I'm looking at that woman on the end. I'm looking at her, watching her, and *seeing* her.

It's her. I know it is.

My throat closes up, and I spin away from the restaurant and practically run across the road, not even looking to see if there are cars coming. Someone honks at me. I hear someone yell, but I keep going, my eyes wide open but unseeing as I finally collapse down on a bench, my back to Tito's.

"Jesus, Collette, you almost died." Jackson stands in front of me for a moment before he turns and sits down next to me. "Are you okay?"

My body feels chilled. I force myself to take a deep breath, then another, then to swallow like that's going to help me speak.

"It's her."

I know it, know it better than I know myself. I don't know what it is about her, the woman in the corner in the tight black top, but it's her. It's Courtney.

"Are you sure?" He turns around to glance back at Tito's

for a second. Fear shoots through me that Courtney might see him, but he's looking at me a moment later, concern etched all over his face. "Are you absolutely sure? She's not someone who looks like Courtney?"

"No, I know it's her."

How could I ever be wrong? As soon as Jackson pointed her out, it was so obvious. Without him here, I might have waltzed on by the window and never given her a second look. I could be two blocks away by now, still hoping I was going to see her but not knowing that I missed my chance.

"You're absolutely sure?" He frowns, a small crease appearing between his eyebrows. There's a smile on his lips, there for a second.

Then it's gone.

Is he laughing at me? I can't bear the thought. My stomach lurches as I try to get into his head and see what he's thinking. "Do you not believe me?" My voice is loud. Too loud.

An elderly couple walking by pauses to look at the two of us.

"No, Collette, of course I do. I want you to make sure. You know you have to be completely sure about this."

It hits me then. He never really believed me. He brought me here to make me see that Courtney is really dead. I stand up, wiping my hands on my jeans. Now I'm frustrated, having figured him out.

"Thank you for your help," I say stiffly. "I'll see you next week in group."

"Collette, I'm sorry, I only wanted —"

"I'll see you next week." I give each word its full weight, wanting him to see that I'm serious. "Thank you for your help."

He sighs and scrubs a hand down his face before nodding

and standing up. "Okay, Collette. I'll see you next week. Are you sure you don't want me to walk you to your car?"

"I'll be fine." What he doesn't realize is that I'm not going to my car. I'm going to wait right here after he leaves until Courtney finishes her meal and her wine, and then I'm going to follow her home.

7

AMANDA

Tito's might be ruined for me forever, and I can't help but admit to myself that it's all my fault if that happens. Joe's staring at me, waiting for me to answer his question even though I'm sure the expression on my face should have told him everything he needed to know.

I take so long to respond that he decides to repeat it.

"Shall we continue this party at my place or your place?"

God. How do I find myself in these situations? He was supposed to be a nice guy, but Beth really glossed over the truth on that one. Sure, he's handsome, but he's the kind of handsome that lets men think they can do whatever they want because their genes blessed them with a symmetrical face.

"You know, I'm not feeling too great," I tell him, which isn't a total lie. I pregamed a bit before this date so I'd feel more confident about meeting someone new, but then I had two glasses of wine to make it through the tapas.

No, I'm not blaming the tapas. The tapas were perfect, like they always are. It's Joe.

"Really? Man, that's unfortunate. I thought we could hang

out and have some more fun." He shrugs like he's letting it roll off his back. "At least you introduced me to this awesome place. I never would have stopped in here on my own, but I'm definitely coming back."

Wonderful. Not only did I go on a terrible date, but I helped him fall in love with my favorite restaurant. I pull some cash from my wallet and throw it down among our plates, wanting more than anything to leave here before he asks me on another date.

"Have a great rest of your weekend," I tell him, scooting my chair back and slipping out before he can do the same. Then I do something that's totally unlike me.

I flee.

Never once in my career have I run away from a problem. If I've had a really sick patient, I've dealt with it. When I've had issues with another doctor, I've gone to them and handled it like a professional. When I have to deliver bad news, I take a deep breath, remind myself that everyone dies eventually, then tell them the truth as kindly as possible.

But right now I'm running. Dr. Amanda Morgan, MD, is running for the door like the devil himself has taken up residency in Tito's.

As soon as I step outside, I suck a deep breath into my lungs and sag against the side of the building in relief. Even with the sidewalks packed today, it still feels less claustrophobic out here than it did in there. I read this morning that there's an antique show down at the end of Main Street, and that's probably where all of these people are headed.

Shrugging my purse higher on my shoulder, I join the crowd for a block before I step to the side. It's not that the day is wasted, exactly, but I don't think I'm going to be able to really enjoy myself after what happened in Tito's. A bad date is one thing. A bad date in my favorite restaurant is reason enough to go home, curl up with a book, and forget this ever happened.

Turning, I cast my eyes around the crowd as I make my way back to my car. Working as an oncologist has its perks, but I'm not in the mood to run into any of my patients or their families. Once I'm in my car, I sigh, crank the AC, then turn my music down to a soft hum as I slowly back out onto Main Street.

There's a crappy little red car waiting on me, and I wave it on, hoping they'll move ahead of me so I can have more space to back out. After upgrading last year I questioned if I really needed something as big as this Navigator, but I like feeling safe and lifted high off the road.

It's bulky to bring downtown, but it's shiny and new, and I love the heated leather seats.

The red car doesn't move.

"Come on," I mutter, plastering a smile on my face as I twist around in my seat to wave them on. I can't see the driver thanks to a shadow across their windshield, but I can imagine whoever it is staring at me and judging me for moving so slowly. I inch out a bit, then a bit more, then press down hard on the gas, swinging out in front of the car before throwing the Navigator into drive.

It follows right behind me, so far up on my bumper I can't see its headlights.

"Stupid tourists. They come here every time we have a big event downtown and then drive like they have their heads caught in their sphincters." Making a right off Main Street, I gun it, glad to put the craziness of the crowds and the bad memory of the date behind me.

There's a flash of red in my rearview mirror, but I ignore it.

Gloria Estefan comes on the radio, and I crank her up, rolling down my windows and letting my hair down from its ponytail. I'm singing, trying to hit the same high notes she can, when I come to a red light and self-consciously turn the radio down.

There's a few cars ahead of me. I doubt I'll make it through this light. Sighing, I glance in my rearview mirror.

It's habit, that's all it is. But I can't help but frown when I see a little red car back there.

"Are you following me?" It's an insane thing to ask. First, there's no way the driver can hear me. Second, just because it *looks* like the same car that was behind me on Main Street doesn't mean it is. There are plenty of little red cars in town, I'm sure of it. I've never looked for them before, so they've never popped out at me.

There's a law about that. You only see the things you're looking for; otherwise, if you're not looking, they become invisible to you.

The light turns green.

Fear makes me grip the steering wheel tighter. This isn't a huge city, not like Chicago or Houston, where you'd almost expect to be followed by a crazy person from time to time, but that's not to say it doesn't happen. Sure, we boast about our low crime rate and how willing everyone is to help a neighbor when they need assistance, but there are crazy people everywhere in the world, and there could be one right behind me.

I'm inching forward. I was right; I'm going to get caught at this light.

My right signal light is clicking for me to turn, but as the light turns red, I press down on the gas and blow through the stop, gritting my teeth and closing my eyes for a moment as I pray that nobody slams into me from either side.

I make it through.

Someone honks their horn, and I give a small apologetic wave while shrinking down in my seat. Hopefully it's not a patient or a colleague, who will call me out on my driving when I see them in the office again, but even if someone says something, I'm going to stand up for myself.

Someone was following me.

I had to shake them.

Of course, the most common advice you always hear is to head straight to the police department, that they'll surround your car and make sure nothing bad happens to you. But I'd dare anyone who thinks they're being followed to make the smartest decision in the moment.

My neighborhood is right up ahead. In my purse, my phone buzzes, but I don't lean over to see who it was. I'm too busy scanning the road in front of me and looking in my rearview mirror to make sure that little red car isn't back.

I start the turn. It's not a gated community, but it's still one of the nicer areas in town. Nobody would dare follow me in here, right?

Still, my heart flips in my chest when I see a red car crest the hill behind me. I let off the gas for a moment, wanting to slow my turn so I can get a good look at the car, make sure it's not the same one that was behind me on Main Street, make sure I'm not really being followed.

As I do, a car strikes the side of my vehicle, spinning me around, slamming my head down so it smacks into the steering wheel. A hot, acrid smell fills the air as the airbag deploys, and I throw my hands up as it hits me; then I'm pinned back against the headrest as my car slows to a stop.

8

COLLETTE

I lost her.

Of course I lost her.

There wasn't any way to pit her nice new car against my beater Honda and think for a moment that I was going to come out on top. Not only did I lose her, which is bad enough that I want to cry, but I'm pretty sure she realized she was being followed.

She saw me, she had to. What else in the world would explain her suddenly running to her car before I had a chance to make it to mine? I didn't even have a chance to tail her home, and now I don't know where she lives.

I won't be able to watch her like I wanted to.

My throat is tight, and I force myself to take a deep breath, inhaling and exhaling as I bend down, pressing my nose against my knees.

Carol suggested yoga when Arabella died, and although I'd scoffed at the idea at first, I have to admit that I like it. I breathe more, feel like I can really inhale and fill my lungs, and I like to think I'm not nearly as frustrated as I was in the past.

But maybe that's all in my head.

Stepping out into warrior pose, I lift my head up and back, feeling the stretch all through my body.

Inhale.

Exhale.

This is supposed to be my time to relax and focus on me, and what do I keep thinking about? Courtney Barrow. I know it was her, knew it from the moment I saw her sitting at the window in Tito's. She's changed some, changed the style of her hair and wears less makeup now, but it's still the same person.

You can work hard to shine a piece of shit, but you'll never turn it into a diamond. That's how the saying goes, isn't it?

"Something like that," I mutter, bringing my hands down flat by my foot before stepping it back next to my other foot. A moment later I'm pressed up into down dog; then I drop down, my triceps burning as I move into Chaturanga.

"But I know it was you," I mutter. My face flames when I think about how she cut out of the crowd on Main Street and ran to her car before I could follow her. "You wouldn't have run if you weren't afraid of me catching on to you. You did this to yourself."

Forcing myself to hold the pose longer than I normally do, I finally press back onto my knees, moving into child's pose. It's comfortable and gives me a moment to really think about what I need to do next.

"Step one," I say, my voice tight from the pressure of my knees on my lungs, "find out where she lives or works."

I take a deep breath and shakily exhale.

"Step two, find out how she's managed to hide for so long."

I need to hold this pose for another minute, and I'll be able to leave my mat and finish up my afternoon. I don't have plans, don't want to see anyone, and even though spending hours tied to my computer looking for Courtney wouldn't be something Carol would advise, I already know what I'm going to be doing.

"Step three," I say, then wait for inspiration to hit me.

Honestly, I'm not sure what step three is going to entail. I know I can't let Courtney get away with having a new life when she should be in prison for what she did to Arabella, but how am I going to do that? I have to somehow convince everyone else that not only is she not dead, but she's actually living her best life while my poor sister is rotting in the ground.

"How hard can it be? I'll follow her, see where she lives and works, and then do some research. She's smart, but I'm smarter."

The words ring hollow in my ears, and I'm not sure if they're true, so I push off the ground and start rolling up my mat before I stop, leaving it on the floor instead. No, even though I like to keep my apartment clean and picked up, it's probably best to leave this out for now. I might need more mat time later to keep myself as calm as possible.

If I have the mat out, then I'm more likely to jump back on it when I'm stressed than to turn to something like the vodka hiding in the back of the cupboard above my refrigerator.

I'm being smart.

Sighing, I stretch, then head over to my computer. Once I have an idea of what I want to do, there isn't much that can stop me. Thinking about Courtney is only going to drive me nuts if I don't jump into my search for her right away.

While my computer warms up, I go to the kitchen and make a cup of tea. By the time I return with my Earl Grey, my computer is up and running and ready for me. The first thing I do is delete a few emails; then I pop over to the local news website to see if anything's going on.

Maybe an intrepid reporter discovered the truth about Courtney without me. Maybe someone out there has already realized what I figured out, and she's under arrest for Arabella's murder. Hope rises in me while the page loads.

The main article is about how schoolteachers need more supplies to teach their classes. There's a supply drive going on at the library, and I've already accepted a bag of notebooks and pencils, so I ignore the headline, looking under that article for anything else of interest.

"Oh, a three-car accident," I say, clicking the headline. I barely read the article, already searching for any pictures that might be included with it. As long as everyone is okay, then it's fine to be a looky-loo.

At least, that's what I tell myself.

No pictures. I sigh, then do a quick search on the website for Courtney Barrow and anything related to my sister's death.

Nothing.

"The vultures have moved on, I see," I mutter, then turn off my computer. As much as I'd like to be able to zone out and enjoy something mindless for an hour or so, I can't. Ever since losing Arabella, I need to keep moving. Either I'm at work or I'm at home doing my yoga or a fitness video, running, cooking...something.

Grief group isn't until Wednesday, and I don't work until Monday morning. As much as I'd like to have something to do this weekend to take my mind off seeing Courtney but not being able to get to her, there's only one thing that will do it for me.

I reach up to the cupboard above the fridge, and I grab the vodka.

9

COLLETTE

One of my favorite things about working in the library is being in the building before all of the patrons arrive and being able to spend time surrounded by stories. Anyone who hasn't spent much time in a library recently is missing out; if you aren't there, you have no idea how magical a place it really is.

There are stories in a library about everything. They whisper to me as I walk among the stacks, putting books back where they belong, carefully making sure they're all tucked nice and neat on the shelves. I like to run my fingers along their spines as I walk through the stacks, imagining what it would be like to pull each one out and disappear into a new world for a while.

In the back of the library, I like to be in charge of book surgery. When a book comes in a little too loved after a visit to someone's home, I make sure to tape it all up, glue back what needs to be glued, do everything necessary to keep the book looking its best. I'm good at it, and that's where I am right now, the tip of my tongue stuck out as I concentrate on fixing the binding.

"That's a really old book," Sara says, carrying a stack of newspapers into the back and dropping them on the table next to me. "You don't have to worry about making it look perfect."

"Sure I do. It's a classic." I flip the cover shut so she can see it's by Judy Blume. "Every girl reads this one growing up, and there's no way I'm giving up on it."

"Whatever you say." She taps the stack of newspapers to force me to look at them. "That kid working on the giant papier-mâché project for his art class is going to swing by after school today and grab these. Leave them here for him, okay? I know you like to clean, but don't toss them."

"You got it." I'm speaking to Sara but staring at the stack of papers. Her hand still rests on the top of it, but right under her fingers I can see newsprint eyes peeking out at me.

Eyes I recognize.

My heart starts to beat faster. I could push Sara's hand off the stack to see more of the photo, but I don't want her to wonder what's wrong with me. Instead, I force myself to smile at her. "I'll leave them right here, okay? And as soon as I'm finished with this Judy Blume, I'll put it back on the shelf and head over to the computer desk to help out anyone there who needs me."

"Great. Thanks." Sara throws me a smile.

Her hand is still on the stack.

"I was wondering, I have a girls' night on Wednesday. We play bunco, and our regular fourth is gone, do you want to join?"

My mind races. *Why won't she leave so I can look at the newspaper?* "I'd love to, but I have group that night."

"Group?" Her eyebrows knit together.

"Grief group. Not like Alcoholics Anonymous or anything, not that there's anything wrong with that. It's grief group. Because of my sister."

"Your sister." She pauses. "Right. Well, if you change your mind and decide that you're feeling up to it by then, let me know. Otherwise, I'm going to ask Ashley over in circulation. She tends to be too serious sometimes, but we need people to take this seriously."

The look she gives me tells me that she regrets asking me. I'm obviously not going to take bunco seriously if I'm thinking about skipping it to go to grief group.

"You do that," I tell her. "I'm busy."

She doesn't say anything, and I wait, frozen where I stand, until the door closes behind her, shutting off the low hum of people talking in the main part of the library.

Only then do I allow myself to look down at the pile of paper. The newspapers are in a messy stack, none of them nice and neat the way they are when they are delivered to us in the morning. Some of them are folded in half, there are a few tears along the top, and they're all bent and mangled from being passed hand to hand as patrons shared them.

But that doesn't bother me. The thing that I can't tear my eyes away from is the woman on the top page. It's an ad for the local hospital, a monthly thing they do to showcase a particular doctor. The plan is to make people feel more comfortable coming in and sharing their health secrets with a stranger.

But right now that's the last thing I'm thinking about.

I know this woman's eyes. I saw them Saturday as she sat in Tito's Tapas and stared out at everyone on Main Street like she was better than them.

But I know more than just her eyes. I know the way her lips curl up in her best approximation of a smile. How cruel she really is behind that smile. The only thing I don't know about this woman is her name, but that's going to be easy for me to change.

"I found you," I say, sitting down for the first time since

arriving at the library that day. My legs feel weak, and I grab the paper, smoothing it out on the table in front of me, Judy Blume temporarily forgotten. "You hid and changed your name, you did everything you could to disappear, but I found you."

For a few minutes I stare at her face. I need to read the write-up from the hospital and see what they're saying about a murderer, how they're spinning the fact that she got drunk and killed my sister, but first I'm staring at her. Drinking her in.

I can't seem to get enough of her.

Finally, when it feels like I've burned her image into my brain, I let myself look down at the words under her picture.

Amanda Morgan, a board-certified oncologist, is considered an expert in her field. She consistently offers the best possible care to her patients, providing them with the knowledge that only comes after years of experience and the compassion they need to feel better while they fight cancer. Not only is she at the forefront of our cancer center, but she spends time on the weekends volunteering and adding to her already busy schedule by helping local community groups. While nobody wants to have to see an oncologist, Amanda is the best in the area and offers all the skills and resources her patients need to feel their best.

When I finish reading, I pause, transfixed by the woman's face. This is too good to be true. I knew I'd seen her, I knew Courtney had been sitting right there at Tito's, and here's my proof.

The only thing is that she's changed her name, but that's not hard. There are a myriad of reasons why women change their name every day, and while it's normally only the last name, I'd wager that with enough reason and money, you could easily change your first name, too.

Reaching down, I pat my pocket for my phone, pulling it out and immediately navigating to do an internet search.

First: how hard is it to change your first and last name?

Second: cancer symptoms and a referral to an oncologist.

I have to make an appointment to see this woman. *Amanda Morgan.* She's a lie. Everything about her is a lie. She's not this incredible oncologist, and she certainly isn't someone other people should look up to. She's a murderer, plain and simple.

Before I know what I'm doing, I rip the article about her out of the paper and tuck it into my pocket, folding it up carefully so her face is on the inside, where it won't smear when it rubs against the fabric of my pants.

I have to expose her. I have to do something to her, even though I'm not entirely sure yet what that is.

But not knowing what my plan is doesn't matter right now because I know who she is. It was a shock seeing her face right here on the paper, but it was also a blessing. I can take time to figure out what I'm going to do, because it's pretty clear she's not going anywhere for a while.

Now I know where Courtney went, and she can't hide from me any longer.

She has no idea, but I'm coming for her.

10

AMANDA

The stares I'm getting because I have my arm in a sling are starting to grow old. It's Tuesday, and I thought all the excitement about my injury would die down yesterday, but I was wrong. Already today I've been stopped half a dozen times by people wanting to know what happened to me or by coworkers asking me if the accident was my fault.

No, it wasn't my fault.

I mean, yes, I'd had something to drink on my terrible date, but that never even came up. I always make sure to stay well below the legal limit; it's something I pride myself on. My career is important to me, and there's no way I'm ever going to throw it away on a technicality like one too many glasses of wine.

I told the police that something had run in front of me and that's why I was slowly turning across incoming traffic. It didn't matter that none of the witnesses who stopped to see what happened for three cars to get into an accident saw anything. The only thing that mattered is that I, a well-known and highly respected oncologist, said that I didn't want to hit whatever it was.

I told them it was probably a dog, but I'd thought it was a kid. It had been easy in the moment, I lied, to make the decision to let myself be involved in an accident rather than risk hitting a child. I wasn't at fault. I was a goddamn hero.

Even so, I can't shake the thought that someone was following me. No, scratch that — I *know* someone was following me. The fact that the red car that crested the hill behind me and made me slow down enough to cause an accident probably hadn't been the same one from Main Street is irrelevant. I was followed, I got scared, and then I messed up.

But it won't happen again. There are only so many main roads here in town, so of course I'm going to have to share them with other people. I might like a plague of locusts not want to, but those are the breaks, and chances are really good that the driver of the red car and I were simply fleeing downtown and all of the tourists who had descended on it.

I shake my head, trying to clear my thoughts. No matter what television shows and movies might have me believe, nobody is out there to hurt me, and it's best if I stop thinking that way.

Besides, if they were really following me, wouldn't they have run the red light when I did? Someone who's tailing you doesn't give up the chase. At least, that's what I've learned from action movies, and I'm choosing to believe it's true.

My favorite radiologist, Dr. Harris, leans in to my office, rapping her knuckles lightly on the doorframe to draw my attention. "You feeling okay?"

"Better than ever," I say, shaking my head so I can focus on her and not on my accident. Of course it happened right after a failed first date. Of course it happened right when I was creeped out by the idea of someone following me. I could blame half a dozen people and events for what happened to me, but I was still the one behind the wheel, and now I'm the one driving a rental this morning.

"Great, listen. I have some mammogram scans from a new patient for you to look at. She's really active, really healthy, and quite honestly, this came as a surprise. She only agreed to the mammogram thanks to a family history of cancer, and she's in shock. I know you're about to go grab some lunch, but do you mind coming by and offering her a few words of encouragement? She's young, and I think it would really help."

"How young?" I'm already on my feet, coming around my desk.

"Thirty-five."

I wince. Too young to be facing this.

"Kids?"

"Twin boys. They're in pre-K."

Any thoughts I'd had about lunch fly out the window as I follow Dr. Harris to where I can meet her patient. Yes, I'm hungry, and yes, I have a full day ahead of me, but this poor woman is in for a world of hurt, and I'm going to be there for her. One thing I pride myself on is treating all of my patients like family. Besides, the sooner we catch something and start treatment, the better the outcome.

Two hours later, I'm juggling a Styrofoam tray loaded down with a baked potato and chili on my way back to my office. My meeting with Dr. Harris's patient — my patient now — went on longer than I thought it would, and then the cafeteria was slammed. I only have twenty minutes to eat something before I have my next patient, so I bump my hip into my office door to throw it open, then kick it carefully shut behind me.

The smell of jasmine makes me freeze.

Slowly, without moving my body, I look around my office. There's nothing here out of the ordinary, nothing that would make me think something was wrong, but that jasmine smell is undeniable and overwhelming.

Carefully, like I need to move slowly to prevent anything bad from happening, I put my tray down on my desk, then turn in a slow circle. Someone was definitely in here. The cleaning staff doesn't wear perfume. They know better than to go into a patient's room wearing a scent as strong as this, as it can cause problems if the patient is sensitive.

So who was in my office?

I pull out my chair and sit down. Nothing different with my chair, but when I really look at my desk, I can see that things have been moved. My notebook, which I always keep on the right side of my desk, with a pen on top, has been shifted towards the middle of my workspace. My cup of cold coffee is turned like someone picked it up, sniffed it, and put it back down.

There's a family picture on the back corner of my desk, a slightly grainy and out-of-focus shot from when I was a little kid at the beach. I'm there with my brother, both of us covered in sand and pink from the sun, grinning next to a starfish we found. That's scooted forward on my desk.

"Someone was in here," I say, pushing back so hard that my chair hits the wall behind me.

Ignoring the food on my desk or how hungry I was a moment ago, I cross my office and throw the door open, marching straight down the hall to the nurses' station. They're not supposed to act like guard dogs, but I know these women.

They love to chat about everything going on in the hospital.

You want to know which doctor is sleeping with which nurse? Ask a nurse.

You're curious about the background of a particular patient? Ask a nurse.

There's some juicy gossip you've only caught snatches of in the doctors' lounge? You know what to do.

"Hey," I say, leaning on their desk and trying to look as calm as possible even though my stomach is doing somersaults, "did you girls see anyone going in my office?"

There's two of them, matching blondes, both of them younger than you would think possible to be a nurse. In between them is a plate loaded with cookies. I spot a few different kinds, and I'm not surprised that there are crumbs all over the desk.

"Someone brought us cookies," the first blonde says, gesturing down at the plate. "I'm sorry, Dr. Morgan, we haven't really been paying much attention to what's going on around us with these beauties here."

"Want one?" The second blonde holds up the plate, frowning at me when I shake my head.

"You didn't see anyone go in my office?"

"Well..." It's the second blonde again. She has chocolate smeared on her lower lip and blushes when I tap my own mouth to point it out. After she rubs it away with a napkin, she continues, "I ran to the cafeteria to grab some napkins and some milk."

Now I see the half-empty glasses of milk on the desk.

"And you?" I turn to the first blonde, who has now turned a satisfying shade of bright red. "Did you leave the desk as well?"

"I didn't mean to, but I thought some of the cleaning staff would like to come join us for cookies."

"Some of the cleaning staff?" Frustration bubbles in me, and I try my best to suppress it, but it's really difficult right now when dealing with these two dumb blondes. "You mean Miguel?"

She nods, somehow turning even redder.

"So someone dropped off cookies, you two scattered like

mice, and that allowed a person or persons unknown to enter my office?" I'm not even trying to hide my frustration right now. My voice is rising as I speak, and I plant my good hand on my desk.

"Did you lock your door?" It's the second blonde, trying a Hail Mary pass to get out of trouble. She wilts when I turn my gaze on her.

"I didn't know I'd need to, not when you two are supposed to know everything that's going on around here."

"Was anything taken?" First blonde this time.

"Does it matter?" I want to yell at the two of them, and I have to fight to keep my voice even. There aren't a lot of patients in this part of the hospital, although there are a few in the rooms behind the nurses' desk. Still, the last thing I need is a reputation for yelling.

"If nothing was taken, then you don't need to be so upset." The first blonde, emboldened now by the fact that nothing actually went missing, pops a bite of cookie in her mouth. "Is there anything else, Doctor?"

I'm shaking when I turn away from them and stalk back to my office. There, I throw my lunch in the trash. I could push this, I know it. I could go to the CEO and tell them there's a problem, or I could talk to the head of nursing. It wouldn't take much of a stink for me to land the two of them in serious disciplinary trouble and have them written up for leaving the desk unattended.

But the only thing I would gain — beside some satisfaction — would be the joy of being ostracized. That's definitely not something I want to deal with, not when my job is already so stressful. Sighing, I sink into my chair, leaning my head back and closing my eyes so I can count to ten in the dark.

Maybe I'm making it all up. I have been under a lot of stress, what with the very nature of my job and the fact that my weekend didn't exactly go the way I wanted it to. Getting in an accident can mess with your mind, and as much as I hate to admit that it's a possibility, it could be that the stress of my accident has me coming apart at the seams.

But then I remember the red car that wouldn't move out of the way on Main Street and the terrible feeling I had when I was convinced it was following me. I'm a doctor, and I breezed through medical school, but I believe in trusting your gut. *Funny tummy feelings* we called them in middle school. They're a real thing.

You know what's not real?

Coincidences.

The car not letting me back out on Main Street combined with the car following me, the changes in my office, and the smell of jasmine...it's too much of a coincidence. I'm a doctor. I don't believe in coincidences. The problem with that belief is the fact that the alternative is upsetting.

It means someone is stalking me. It means they know where I work; they were in my space.

It means I need to be careful.

11

COLLETTE

I'm so fidgety during grief group that it's hard for me to concentrate. We have a new member, an older man who lost his daughter. He's here alone, his wife refusing to come join him, but even though I know I should feel bad for him and offer him more attention while he's talking, I can't wait until group is over so I can talk to Jackson.

I want to tell him what I know. Of course, I'll leave out the part where I tried to follow Courtney home from Main Street. That makes me sound unhinged, but I'm definitely not, and it's not like I managed to do it anyway, so why mention it? I want the truth to finally come out, for my sister to receive justice for her death.

Vince looks around the group, then asks us to bow our heads in prayer.

I do, but not before casting a quick glance around the room. Gavin stares openly at me, and I blink at him before dropping my gaze and folding my hands in my lap. Growing up, Arabella and I went to Catholic school, so going through the motions of prayer while really thinking about something more entertaining is nothing new to me.

I should listen harder to Vince, but I gave up on God a long time ago. As soon as we all say *Amen*, some of us with more meaning than others, I'm out of my seat, my legs and hips sore from sitting there for so long. There's already a crush of people around the snack table, and I hang back, not wanting to seem too eager to talk to Jackson.

He's speaking with the new man, their two heads bowed together. Keeping an eye on them, I pour myself some coffee and grab a donut. They look stale, and I'm not surprised that I choke on the first bite. Washing it down with coffee so strong I'll be up for hours, I eyeball Jackson, waiting for him to become available.

He's animated, but so is the new man. I squint, trying to make out his name tag. *Walter.*

"Checking out the new guy?" Gavin's next to me, taking a sip of his coffee while he eyeballs me over the Styrofoam edge. "He's too old for you, don't you think?"

"I want to see his name." Talking to Gavin flusters me. It's not that I find him attractive, not at all; only that I heard him talking to Jackson last week about how what I felt wasn't really possible. That's enough to make anyone wary of speaking to another person. "I wanted to talk to Jackson, but he's busy."

"You can talk to me."

I grimace.

"So, are you feeling better, Collette?" he queries. "Still having intrusive thoughts and bad dreams?"

This is not happening. There isn't anyone here I dislike more than Gavin, and to have to talk to him and pretend I care what he's saying is enough to get my hackles up. Instead of responding or telling him to leave me alone, I turn on my brightest smile. "Everything's fine, Gavin. Thanks for worrying about me."

He grins. This is a game to him. I don't know why, but for

some reason, Gavin wants to play a game with me. Unfortunately for him, I'm not interested.

"I looked up your sister. The drunk driver is dead."

I'm halfway through turning away from him, but what he says makes me freeze in place, and I slowly turn back, my eyes searching his face for any sign of laughter.

He's not kidding.

"You what?" There's venom in my voice now, and I don't make any effort to disguise it. "You looked up Arabella?"

He nods.

My hand itches to smack the self-satisfied grin off his face, but I can't be kicked out of group. Part of my agreement with my therapist to stop seeing her regularly was to transition to a group setting where I could still be supported without the pressure of it being one-on-one. There's no way I'm going to risk losing that.

"Why would you do that?"

"You seemed so convinced that the drunk driver was still alive, and I wanted to check. I wanted to help you, Collette, nothing more, nothing less."

"And now you think I'm crazy?"

He doesn't have time to respond before Jackson turns to the two of us. He smiles, and it's not like the heavens open up or anything, but I feel myself relax. Jackson isn't someone I'm interested in, but I feel like he understands me, and that's worth something.

Brushing past Gavin without waiting for him to respond, I tap my cup of coffee against Jackson's in greeting, then tilt my head towards the door. "Ready to go?"

"You got it. In a rush to leave?"

"Definitely." It's still warm outside, the night definitely creeping in, but mostly held at bay by the parking lot lights. A few moths are already swirling around, and I turn away from them, stepping back from Jackson so I can get a better look at him. "Listen, that woman we saw at Tito's? In the front window?"

He nods, an interested expression on his face.

Do I sound deranged? I exhale, brushing some of my hair back from my face. Ever since trying to follow her home and then finding her write-up in the newspaper at work Monday, I've felt like I'm going insane.

Not to mention what I did yesterday. That's something I don't think I can tell Jackson about. Trying to follow someone home is one thing. Bribing nurses to break into someone's office is another entirely.

"That's Courtney. The girl who killed Arabella, I know it is."

Jackson exhales hard, tilting his face up to the sky. "Collette, are you sure?"

"Of course I'm sure. I wouldn't have done what I did if I weren't sure." *Crap.*

His head snaps back down, and he stares at me. "What did you do?"

"I looked into her." Raising one shoulder, I drop it, trying to look casual. "I looked into her, Jackson. She's alive; she changed her name."

"And you learned all of this simply by looking into her?"

After glancing over my shoulder to make sure nobody who might overhear us is coming out of the building, I lower my voice, stepping closer to Jackson. As quickly as possible and trying to seem as rational as possible, I explain everything.

How I may have tried to follow her home before I lost her. How I saw her face in the paper on Monday at the library. How I went to her office with cookies and snuck past the two nurses outside her office. It sounds terrible when I say it out loud, and I see how his eyes narrow, but he doesn't interrupt me. It's only when I'm finished and I drop my hands down to my sides with a loud clap that he speaks.

"You could go to the police about this."

"Oh, no, no, no," I say, cutting him off with a wave of my hand. "No police. You want to know why? Because they already told me she's dead. They told me *over and over*. It didn't matter who I spoke to at the department. Do you want to know what the police really hate?"

He cocks an eyebrow at me, a clear invitation for me to continue.

"Being wrong. They hate it more than anything, and there's no way I'm going to risk upsetting them by pointing out how wrong they all are."

"So you feel like you need to handle this on your own." It's not a question, but I nod anyway, reaching out and lightly touching him on the shoulder.

"Yes," I breathe. "You understand. I knew you would."

"Oh, Collette." He runs his hand through his hair and sighs, the heavy sigh of someone who knows they must tread lightly with what they say next. "You need to be careful. But if it's really her, then you have to get closer. You have to know for sure."

"I do." It's nice that he sees I'm right, although I knew this already. There's no way I can sit back and relax while Arabella's murderer walks around free. What kind of sister would I be if I did that?

Later, when I'm home alone, I sit in the glow of my computer, working on the most tedious project I've ever completed. I had to pay for a month of Photoshop to be able to do this, but it will all be worth it in the end.

When I finally sit back from my computer, I have a crick in my neck. My printer whirs, and I make myself wait until I grab the paper from its tray.

It's perfect.

12

AMANDA

I'm not a paranoid person, I swear I'm not, but I still look both ways for longer than necessary before pulling out onto the main road on my way to work in the morning. It doesn't make any sense, I know that, but I'd swear on a Bible that I can still smell jasmine even though the only place I smelled it was in my office.

In the end, I hunted down one of the hospital cleaners, begged them for some Lysol spray, and sprayed down every surface in my office. It didn't eliminate the gross feeling I have that someone was in my space, but it did get rid of the smell.

The weekend took care of any lingering jasmine odor. It's now been deep-cleaned by the cleaning staff, not only sprayed with Lysol, and when I was at work yesterday, it felt like everything was back to normal. Even though it's been almost a week since someone was in my space, I still feel violated. It's Tuesday now, though, and I know I need to get over the fact that someone was in my office — and I still don't know who it was.

Beating out a rhythm on my rental's steering wheel, I zip through town, checking my mirrors at every stop and every turn. I don't see any little red cars, but that doesn't mean it's not out here. It doesn't mean the person who I thought was following me isn't around town.

"What's that saying?" I ask, turning down the radio. "You're only crazy if you don't think you are?"

Still, I scan the parking lot when I pull in, taking my time as I make my way around to where the doctors park. Normally I don't do this. I usually take the straightest shot so I can hurry into my office and start my day, but not today. Not until I shake off the uncomfortable feeling I have, like someone is scratching really lightly at the back of my neck.

"Come on, Amanda," I mutter, turning down the last row of cars. "You've lost your mind, and you know it." Still, I drive slowly, my head on a swivel as I work my way through the crowded lot.

And then I see it.

Pulled so far up into its space like it's trying to hide there. The back bumper has a massive dent in it, and I wonder vaguely if the driver backed into something or someone ran into them.

It's a little red car.

Before I know what I'm doing, I'm throwing my new-to-me rental SUV into park and leaping out. The wind whips my coat around me. I pull it closer, trying to stay warm as I hurry around the front of my car to the little red car.

If I hadn't been looking everywhere for a car like this, I doubt I would have even noticed it parked here. It looks like any other old beater you see in a parking lot, but the fact that it's in my parking lot, right outside the hospital where I work, is enough to make me look closer.

Taking a deep breath, I cup my hands around my face and press them up to the side windows.

My heart hammers in my chest. I think for a moment I see movement inside the car, and I jerk back before I realize it's only the distorted shadow of a bird flying overhead. I thought for sure someone was in the front of the car, but I was wrong.

There's a book on the passenger seat, but it's flipped upside down, so I can't tell what the title is. In the cup holders, there's a half-empty water bottle and a lanyard with a badge on it. I twist my neck as hard as I can to see what's on that badge.

Whoever was following me drives this car.

I know it.

"Excuse me!" A man's voice makes me jump, and I jerk back from the window, my face already flaming and hot. "That's my car. Is there a problem?"

"Not a problem," I stutter, taking him in.

I thought he was a man at first, thought for sure he had to be around my age judging by how deep his voice is, but he's a teenager. Given how gangly he is and the acne smattered across his face, I'd say he's a young teenager. Keys dangle from his fingers, and he waves them at me as he stops a few feet from me.

Does he think I'm a cat he can scare off?

"I'm sorry," I say, glancing behind him to make sure none of my coworkers are going to witness this. "I thought I saw something moving in the front seat and wanted to make sure there wasn't a dog or something locked in the car. It could overheat."

I'm well aware of how overcast the sky is, but still. Locking your dog in a car on any day should be a crime.

He visibly relaxes. "Oh, right on, thanks. No, I left Noodle at home. I thought you were breaking in."

"Definitely not. Sorry about that, you have a good day, okay?" I scoot past him, and he moves to the side, turning slightly so I can slip between him and the cars without brushing up against him. My face burns with embarrassment as I hurry across the parking lot and through the hospital to my office.

I don't really stop until I'm sitting at my desk, my head in my hands.

"Oh, God," I whisper, even though there isn't anyone around to hear me. "I looked like an idiot, didn't I?" I'm alone, but it's not like I need anyone to answer that question for me. I know I looked stupid, know he's probably going to shake his head about what I did for the rest of the day, but I couldn't help myself.

The thought that whoever was following me in the red car might be here, in the hospital parking lot, waiting for me to walk by…It was too much for me to bear.

I'm in the middle of looking at my calendar to see what cases I have coming up today when my phone rings. We don't have caller ID at the hospital, and I answer it without questioning who it might be.

"This is Dr. Morgan," I say, finally dragging my eyes away from my calendar. It's a packed day, and I'm going to be really lucky if I manage to make it out the door right at five. Still, that's what I signed up for when I became an oncologist. I'm willing to put in the extra hours to make sure my patients are as well cared for as possible.

"Amanda, it's Dr. Harris. You got a second?"

"For you? Always." I grab a pen and a pad of paper, preparing myself to take notes if needed. Dr. Harris doesn't usually call up to my office unless something important is going on, and I can only imagine what might have inspired her to reach out to me.

"Thanks. Listen, I have this case I want to talk to you about. It's a doozy, and you're the best person I know to offer me good advice on it." She pauses. "If you don't mind, can we meet for lunch?"

"You got it." I pause, then reach out and lightly touch my screen with my finger. "Hey, do you know a Belle Smith?"

"Doesn't ring a bell. Why?"

"She's on my list to see today, but I don't know the referring doctor. No idea where she came from, and I wondered if you'd heard her name from someone else. And I don't have her chart yet, so I can't read up on her." It's not the fact that I don't know the woman that gives me pause. Pretty much every single patient who comes through for me to see is someone I don't know, but usually I recognize the referring doctor. Not being able to put my finger on who it is feels strange for me. I'm also not entirely sure if I should see her without her chart.

She's probably terrified, though, and I never want to leave any patient hanging when they're scared.

"Nope. Might be someone from a smaller town looking for help for their patient. This is what happens when you're the best in the business." She's teasing me, but there's truth in what she's saying. Dr. Harris and I are a dream team together. "Anyway, if you need a consult, let me know once you receive her records. I'll see you at lunch."

"You got it. See you." We hang up, and I stare at the name on my list. She's my first patient to see, right at eight this morning, and I need to get my head on straight after my run-in with the guy in the parking lot.

After all, every patient deserves my best. There's no way I'm going to let down a single one, no matter if I'm feeling a little off that day or not.

13

COLLETTE

My leg bouncing up and down is sure to give away how nervous I'm feeling, so I still it, planting both of my feet on the floor and taking a huge breath. I hate hospitals. Ever since I was little and experienced the antiseptic smell covering up the smell of vomit and death, I've hated them.

And now I've willingly walked into one of them to try to attempt to be closer to the woman who killed my sister. I've waited days for this appointment, and even though I'm nervous, I'm not going to let anything mess it up.

It's a wild idea and definitely not something I was excited to tell Jackson about even though I wanted someone to know where I am and what I'm doing. Honestly, I can only imagine what he might say, which is why I sent him a text telling him what I was doing and then turned my phone off so I wouldn't see if he responded right away.

"Ms. Smith?" The receptionist leaning out into the waiting room is pretty. She has her long red hair pulled back and a swipe of mascara on, making her look younger than she probably is. I smile at her and stand, clutching my purse in front of my body like it's a shield. "If you'll follow me, I'll take you to see Dr. Morgan."

This is it. My heart beats so hard I'm sure she's going to hear it as I pass her in the door, then wait for her to lead the way. It took guts for me to call and pretend to be a doctor's office sending me in for a referral, but it worked. Of course I didn't use my real name, I'm not that stupid, so I have to pay attention when they call me by my fake name.

But now it's all worth it. I'm one step closer to meeting Courtney in person.

I hop on a scale, answer a few questions about my lifestyle habits, then watch as the nurse draws blood. She gives me an encouraging smile that I'm sure is supposed to make me feel better about what's going on, then tells me that Dr. Morgan will be with me momentarily and that I need to sit tight.

So I do, swinging my legs back and forth as I wait. As a rule, I try not to go to the doctor's because I hate everything about it. I hate the waiting in the room. I hate sitting in a crinkly paper gown, but at least I've avoided that this time. Coming to an oncologist is a new experience for me, and I'm interested in how this is going to go.

There's a soft rap on the door, and then it swings open. As soon as the doctor steps in, I feel like all the breath has been snatched from my lungs. Grabbing my thighs, I squeeze hard, letting my nails sink in through my jeans to help me stay focused.

I have to pay attention to everything, have to remember every single detail of meeting her. This is the first time I've been this close to Courtney, and I don't want to forget anything. "Dr. Morgan," I say, putting a smile on my face. I can play this game with her. She wants to go by a new name, so I do, too. Part of me wonders if she'll be able to tell that I'm lying to her like she's lying to me.

"Ms. Smith, why don't you hop off that table and sit here with me?" She gestures at two chairs next to each other. They're pushed against the wall but turned slightly so we'll be able to talk without having to twist to see each other. "I have a lot of questions for you, and I don't want you to feel uncomfortable up on that table."

I have a lot for you, too.

"Sure." Swallowing hard, I slip down from the table and sit in the chair next to her. This close I can see the laugh lines around her eyes. I see how she has a few gray hairs on her temples, how she has them brushed back away from her face, not even worrying about trying to dye them. She's not old, not by a long shot, but she's older than Arabella will ever be, and I hate her for that.

She took Arabella's chance to grow old, and I'll never forgive her.

"We received a call from your doctor's office that you needed to be seen for breast cancer. I asked them to send over your file, but they haven't done that yet." Her voice is soothing. It's like honey, and I realize with a start that I'm leaning closer to her like I'm going to fall into what she's saying.

There's a pause, and it hits me that she's waiting on me to respond.

"That's strange." My voice sounds funny to my ears. It's high and tighter than I'm used to, and I wonder if she notices that something's not right. I clear my throat. "I can reach out to them after I leave here and see what they say."

"Yeah, that would be great. I'll have someone here connect with them too. In fact, they might be calling while you and I are meeting this morning to put things in motion."

I freeze. It had been easy enough to set up a Google phone number and have it forwarded to my phone. But did I turn it off when I got here this morning? I'd come flying in on two wheels, grabbing a parking spot and then practically running to make it to my appointment.

Sweat beads on my forehead, and I wipe it off, trying to look calm.

"Hopefully one of us can reach them soon."

Can I reach down into my purse and check to see if my phone's off? I think I turned it off, but am I making that up?

I have to risk it. Leaning down, I pick my purse up and pull out ChapStick, rubbing it all over my lips.

"Sorry," I say, "I get dry lips when I'm nervous." Slipping it back into the main zipper pocket, I say a hasty prayer as my fingers close around my phone.

"I completely understand. Nerves are rough, and you're going through a lot right now." Reaching out, she rests her hand on my knee.

I stare at her hand before finally peeking inside my purse. My phone is off.

Thank God.

"Yeah, this is unexpected. My mom didn't have cancer. Actually, I don't think anyone in my family has ever had cancer." *Including me.*

"These things happen. A lot of patients look for something or someone to blame, but there's usually no place to put the blame. Genetics are strange, and it's not unsurprising to me that you don't have a cancer history in your family. What matters is that your doctor was able to catch it right away, and now we can figure out how to take care of it. Of course, without all of your information, I can't really speak to your type of cancer, but I can give you an overview of what to expect."

I nod. What else am I going to do? I lied through my teeth to set up this appointment, and now that I'm here, I'm not sure if I've made a stupid decision. It's one thing to want to meet Courtney in person, another for it to actually happen.

She launches into information about treatment options, and I do my best to look like I'm paying attention. Really, though, my mind races as I stare at her. When I saw her through the window at Tito's, I knew for sure that it was her. And now, seeing her up close and in person, I know I'm right.

There's no doubt in my mind. Not that I thought there would be, but still it's nice to have my thoughts confirmed.

"Of course, everything is on hold right now until we receive your file, so some of what I said might change to fit your needs." She stares at me and then shakes her head. "I'm so sorry; I hope you don't feel like you wasted your time coming in here when there's really nothing that I can do for you right now. As soon as everything is sent over, we'll call you back in for another appointment, and we'll be able to come up with a personalized treatment plan for you."

"It's fine." My mouth feels stuffed full of cotton. "I wish they'd been more on top of it. I'm sure you're busy with patients all day long. I should be apologizing to you." I stand up, awkwardly grabbing my purse, but before I can take a step towards the door, she's right there, her hands on my shoulders, staring straight into my eyes.

"You have nothing to apologize for, okay? I want to make sure all of my patients get the care and love they need during this difficult time. Don't you worry about a thing. I'm going to personally reach out to your doctor and see if I can't expedite them sending your information over. When you're facing a health crisis like this, the last thing you need is to be under extra pressure."

God, she's so *nice*.

"Thank you." I need to get out of here, away from the antiseptic smell, away from how she's looking at me. I know you can't look in another person's eyes and read their mind, but it honestly feels like she can.

She lets me go, and I bolt.

I don't slow down until I'm outside. Only then do I pause and turn, looking back at the hospital. It's not like at Tito's where I could see through the glass and watch her without her seeing me. Here, she can easily look out and see me, but I have no idea where she might be.

"How was she that kind?" I ask myself, turning and walking towards my car. "It's not normal."

It's also hard for me to reconcile the fact that someone who could murder my sister while drunk driving could be that nice, but I got what I came for. I know the truth.

It's her. I don't care how caring she seems, what kind of a doctor she is, or who she's become after killing Arabella.

She's Courtney Barrow, hiding in plain sight.

And now that I've found her, I'm not letting her get away from me. Ever.

14

AMANDA

I don't find time to call Ms. Smith's doctor until close to five, and as the phone rings, I mentally cross my fingers that they'll pick up. It's strange that they wouldn't send over her file right away when they called to make the referral, but I know things sometimes are held up, even when you need them in a hurry.

It's not unheard of for an office to make the referral and then send the patient's file later. That's probably what happened with this case, but I can't help Ms. Smith in any way without her information.

The call goes to voicemail, and I leave a message with my number, stressing that it's important they call me back ASAP. It's one thing for a doctor's office to drop the ball, but another for them to continue to drag their feet when I need something for a patient. Hopefully this won't take long.

After that's done, I clean off my desk and lock my office, hurrying downstairs and out the front door. It's supposed to rain tonight, and I want to be home and drinking a glass of wine before the storm hits. After waving at a few doctors I know in the parking lot, I press a button on my key fob to help me locate my car.

It's two rows away, and I head in that direction, walking quickly, already thinking about the glass of wine I'll have with dinner and the bit of tea afterwards.

Then I stop.

There's a flash of red in between the gray and black cars that make up the majority of the vehicles in the parking lot. Standing still for a moment, I eyeball it like I fully expect the car to disappear. But it doesn't.

Turning so I can cut through some cars, I start walking away from where I parked my rental car to the red car. It's small, like the car I saw here before, but surely it isn't...

It is.

"What the hell?" Even though I know what I'm about to do is insane, I rush to the window and cup my hands, pressing my face up against the glass. It's the second time I've done this today, but surely it's not the same car.

Surely it's a coincidence. There have to be hundreds of red cars in town, a number of them with a damaged back bumper, and this is a big hospital.

Still, my heart flips in my chest when I see the stuff in the cup holder. It's the same red car.

Horrified, I back away, looking right and left as I do, hoping that boy isn't going to be watching me like he was this morning. The car is in a different spot, which tells me he left and then came back, but why?

Was he watching me?

The thought gives me chills. I can't seem to move fast enough away from the car, and I hurry, dropping my chin down to my chest so that anyone looking over might not immediately recognize me. Why did I walk over to this car? I should have seen it and then kept going.

I'm almost to my rental, and I fumble the keys from my

pocket. It takes me a moment to find the unlock button on the fob, but then I mash it and hop in, slamming the door behind me and locking myself in as quickly as possible.

There.

Safe.

As soon as I'm in the driver's seat, I chuckle to myself. I've lost my mind. That's literally the only explanation for what happened. There's absolutely no reason for me to be hustling across the hospital parking lot like that, not when I don't know that someone was actually watching me.

Still.

Reaching up, I grab the rearview mirror and adjust it so I can see behind me more clearly. The parking lot may be full of cars, but there aren't a lot of people out here right now. Still, I wait a moment, my heart pounding in my chest.

Nothing.

No person walking up to my car, no boy who I think might be following me. Forcing a laugh, I rub my hands up and down my arms to warm up a bit, then start the vehicle. The engine roars to life in a way I'm still not used to, and I jump, then shake my head.

"You're being ridiculous," I whisper, backing out of my space and heading towards the exit. "You have no idea how many red cars there are in town. It's science — now that you're looking for them, you're going to see them. That doesn't mean there are more of them or that they're actually following you."

Talking to myself makes me feel a bit better.

It's Tuesday, the day I always swing by the cemetery, and even though a voice in my head is screaming at me to skip out on routine and head straight home, I can't seem to do that.

There's a grocery store on the way to the cemetery, and I pull in, now moving on autopilot. It only takes me a moment to grab some flowers and check out; then I'm back in the car and pulling out. All I want is to be in my house, to lock the doors and shut the blinds, but I'm doing this first.

I promised myself I'd go weekly, and I've never missed a trip. There's no way I'm going to start now.

Traffic decreases considerably as I head out of town, and pretty soon I'm the only one on the road. Leaving the main part of the town behind always relaxes me, and I feel my grip on the steering wheel grow loose. I let the car have more control as I take the dips and turns, and shortly I'm pulling up to towering wrought-iron gates.

Closing time is in an hour, and I'll probably be the only person here. That's how it is every week, and I have to say that I usually like it. Today I keep looking behind me for a red car with a damaged back bumper, but there isn't one on the road, and in a few minutes I'm through the gates, have driven down the drive, and parked in an empty lot.

The wrought-iron gates look impressive, but everyone in town knows that Glendale Cemetery doesn't have a fence around it. A few times I've come across a deer that's come in through the back woods to graze among the graves. Bracing myself for the burst of movement and sound they make when startled, I grab my flowers and start the walk.

Five minutes later I'm in front of the same headstone I stand in front of every single week.

"I brought daises this time," I tell my daughter, removing the old flowers from the vase built into the headstone and replacing them with the fresh ones. It rained last night, a storm that sent drops flying against my windows, and the vase still has water in it, so I don't need to worry about filling it up.

"You never really got to know what a daisy is, but I always said I'd teach you to make daisy chains when you got older." There's a lump in my throat as I gather up the plastic the flowers came in. It crinkles loudly in the silent air.

I cast another glance over my shoulder.

"I'm sorry I can't stay long, Greta, but I wanted to stop by. Wanted to tell you I'm thinking about you."

She's not here. I know she's not here. I still like to let my daughter know that I'm thinking about her.

All the books I've read have told me that it's okay to do that. It's normal, in fact, to want to have a relationship with the people you lost. Wanting it doesn't mean that it's going to happen, though.

I know that.

"I can't stay long," I repeat, even though the words are just for me. "Things have been weird. I know I can handle them; it's that it's strange to be facing them by myself."

Not that Greta would have been much support. Babies take much more than they give, but I can't help but imagine that she might have given me the support and love I needed, even if it was only because of the routine I'd have had with her.

"Anyway." Clearing my throat, I wipe tears from my eyes. "I miss you. Things are good here, but they'd be better with you. I love you, Greta."

I have to force myself to turn away from the tiny grave-stone and walk back to my car. How many times have I made this exact same trip? It's been years since she died in her sleep as an infant, years since I held her body to my chest and sobbed.

Years since my marriage fell apart, since I got divorced, since I threw myself into my work, into saving people. A shrink would probably tell me that the reason I'm so dedicated to my patients is because I couldn't save my daughter, but I'm not going to give anyone the chance to tell me that.

And as to how many times I've brought flowers here? I guess that I could probably count them all up if I really wanted to know, but the truth is that I'm not sure I do.

Knowing how many times I've come to visit Greta, replaced the flowers I've brought for her grave, and then left again would only depress me. This is something I do. Something quiet, something for me. I'm so preoccupied walking to my car that I almost miss the flash of red as another car pulls out of the parking lot.

Almost.

15

COLLETTE

My heart slams in my chest as I press down harder on the gas, driving fast away from the cemetery. It was probably stupid to follow Courtney in there, but once I saw her leave the hospital, I knew I had to see what she was doing.

What does someone like her know about grief?

Part of me thought for a moment that she must be going to visit Arabella's grave, but I dismissed that thought as insane. There wasn't any way a drunken murderer like her would visit my sister. Sure enough, even though I held back from pulling into the parking lot behind her for longer than I would have liked, I wasn't surprised to see her hurry through the cemetery in the opposite direction from Arabella's grave.

Curiosity got the better of me. I knew it was dangerous, knew it might result in me coming face-to-face with Courtney — or Amanda Morgan, as she pretends to be — but I parked and followed her, staying far enough back that I could easily dart behind a gravestone if she were to turn.

She carried flowers, clutching them like they gave her strength, and I watched in surprise when she stopped at a sweet little headstone, an angel carved in the front, a vase on top. I watched as she changed the flowers; then I hurried back to my car, determined not to let her catch me.

Who in the world was she visiting in the cemetery? The flowers she pulled from the vase on the gravestone were wilted, sure, but they weren't completely dead. They looked like they'd spent some hot days in the sun.

So who put them there? Was it her?

My mind reels with the possibility of why she'd be replacing flowers on a regular basis. If she lost someone dear to her, then I want to feel bad for her. I know what it's like to lose the person you love more than anything and to feel like your entire world is going to fall apart.

But I don't feel any sympathy, not a scrap of it.

After Arabella died, I was in a terrible place. I felt like I couldn't crawl my way out of it, like the darkness pressing down on me was going to be forever. I wanted to climb into the casket with her and be covered up with dirt so I never had to be without my sister again.

But now I'm alive, and I have a mission. I want to seek revenge for Arabella, want to make sure she is remembered the way she deserves to be. Nothing can stop me from doing that.

No, even though I feel for anyone who has lost someone they love, I'm not going to let that change what I'm doing. Finding Courtney and punishing her for what she did to my sister has been my main goal since the accident. How she managed to convince everyone she was dead is beyond me, but I'm not letting her get away with the pain she's caused me.

I'm driving faster now, pressing down harder than is necessary on the gas pedal. Even though I know I should slow down to be safer, I want to put distance between myself and the cemetery. It was uncomfortable going there and not visiting Arabella, but I'll do that later this week.

She'd understand.

Once I hit some of the downtown traffic, I relax, loosening my grip on the steering wheel and exhaling hard. It was stupid to hang around the hospital all day, hoping to see her when she left, but I want to know what she does. I need to know where she goes, whom she spends time with, how she's living her life.

She's lucky enough to have a life after taking my sister's, but that's not going to be the case for much longer.

My mind races while I drive. I think about what it will be like to tell Courtney that her attempt to hide from me failed. I think about how amazing it will be to tell her I hunted her down, that she can't hide any longer, that she's finally going to get what she deserves.

And what is that?

I hear the question in my mind as clearly as if someone sitting in the passenger seat had asked it. Surprised, I actually turn to look next to me to make sure there isn't anyone there.

I'm alone. Tapping my brakes, I let my car slow to a stop at a red light.

That's a really good question.

When I was told that Courtney had killed herself, the first thing I felt was a sense of relief. I'd wanted her to suffer for what she did to my sister.

Then I realized it was all a lie.

I needed to find her to stop her from hurting someone else. To punish her, send her to prison where she belongs.

But up until my walk with Jackson two weekends ago, I haven't been able to find her. I've known she might change her name, change the color and cut of her hair. I've seen enough movies to be aware of how people can hide in plain sight when they want to, and I've been prepared for that.

But now that I found her, what in the world am I going to do?

"I'm going to ruin her life," I announce in the silence of my car. She ruined mine, she ruined Arabella's, and I'm going to make her suffer for every good thing she's been able to enjoy since then. It's the only thing that makes sense to me.

And if I can't make her suffer? If she's somehow untouchable as Amanda Morgan, this incredible doctor whom everyone seems to love?

Well, I already know the answer to that. I might not want to think about it, might not be totally comfortable admitting it to myself, but I already know what I'm going to do.

It's for Arabella.

Everyone will understand.

16

AMANDA

Someone was watching me.

I know it as sure as I know anything else in my life to be true. There was someone at the cemetery who wasn't there when I pulled in, someone who wasn't there very long, and then who pulled out right as I was walking back to my car.

And the clincher? The thing that really tells me that someone is spying on me and that I need to be careful?

That someone was driving a red car. Something isn't right. I don't have to rely on my medical degree or funny tummy feelings to believe that.

Even though it's still warm outside, I'm suddenly freezing, and I crank the heat in the car, rubbing my hands over my arms before grabbing the steering wheel again. Leaving the cemetery is always hard for me. It's emotional to go visit that tiny grave and talk to the daughter I was never lucky enough to know, but this is different.

I don't want to cry over the fact that I lost a baby and never got to know her.

I want to find whoever was watching me and corner them.

I want to scream at them, tell them to stop, find out who they are and what they want. It's not fair that someone is torturing me like this, driving me to the point of distraction.

A love song comes on the radio, and I violently wrench the knob to the left to turn it off.

Silence.

Right now I'm not even sure what I should do. I keep glancing in my rearview mirror, praying that there isn't anyone behind me, praying that whoever might be watching me hasn't somehow looped around me.

There are too damn many red cars in this town. But I don't see one with a dented back bumper. I don't see the boy from the hospital this morning. I've always been useless with makes and models of cars, and they all look the same to me. The only thing that stands out about them is their color, and the bright red is so eye-catching I can't seem to miss it.

"Could it be you?" I whisper the question, slowing down to turn into my neighborhood. Usually I gun it now, wanting nothing more than to hurry home, have a glass of wine, and relax, but I take my time as I drive, giving anyone plenty of time to pull in behind me.

Nothing.

But what would a teenage boy want with me? I rack my brain, trying to think if I've ever met him before. The problem is that I didn't pay much attention to him — apart from clocking his unfortunate skin and awkward gangly limbs. He was nothing, a teenager, someone I didn't expect to see this morning and someone I didn't think I'd ever see again.

But what if he's the one following me? I know people can be creepy, that they can make up a relationship with a person in their mind, convincing themselves that there's something real between them and the object of their fantasy. I have no idea if that's something this boy might have done, or if that scenario's even a possibility.

All I know is that someone has been following me, and he might be doing it. It's creeping me out, the thought that someone is learning my schedule, and even though I'm right in front of my driveway and should pull in and lock the doors, I keep the steering wheel steady and straight and drive on.

There's a cul-de-sac at the end of the neighborhood — one way in, one way out. I drive around it faster than I probably should and have a very strong feeling I'm going to find a notice in my mailbox about slowing down.

Whatever. At this point, my neighbors can assign a neighborhood watchdog to tail me. At least then I'd have someone else looking out for me.

Now I'm back at the entrance to my neighborhood. Part of me is excited that I didn't run into anyone trying to tail me on the way to my house, the other part of me is disappointed. I don't want there to be anyone stalking me, but if there is, then I'd rather know about it now than later.

I have to pull into a neighbor's driveway and then back out to turn around and go home. My face heats when she walks out onto the porch, shielding her eyes with her hand to look at me.

Groaning, I roll down my window and lean out. "Sorry, Mrs. Ketcham," I call, hoping she'll recognize me even though I'm in a rental. "I thought I had to run to the store and then remembered that I have what I need at home!"

She rolls her eyes, *rolls her eyes*, then flaps her hand at me like she's dismissing me.

"Whatever, you old witch," I mutter, gritting my teeth and smiling at her while I back down her driveway. "I bet you're loads of fun at a party."

A few minutes later I'm in my garage. Normally I'd hop right out and head into the house, but I wait in my locked car until the door drops all the way behind me. Only then do I hop out and rush to the door to let me into the kitchen. It only takes me a minute to turn off the alarm, lock the door behind me, and turn the alarm back on.

Sighing with relief, I sag against the door.

If you're not safe in your own house, then where the hell will you be safe? I've always thought that my home would be my fortress, the one place I could exist without ever being afraid of anything, but right now I'm beginning to question how true that thought actually is. I have an alarm system. Supposedly I live in a neighborhood with a great neighborhood watch group who will keep an eye on everything.

What I've found, though, is that mostly translates to nosy neighbors who hate it when you make any loud noises in your own backyard.

I've lived my entire life doing everything I can to mitigate risk and to ensure my own safety. Still, I lost my baby. Still, I feel creeped out by someone following me.

The only thing that will help right now is wine, and I finally push away from the door, head to the kitchen, yank open the fridge, and take a sip straight from the bottle. That's a habit I picked up in college, when my roommate and I were too poor to buy anything decent. The wine we drank would taste like vinegar if left open for very long.

Now I don't have that problem, but I still take a sip, still close my eyes for a moment when the alcohol spreads across my tongue. I don't want to rely on wine to survive the evening. Isn't that a cliché — a doctor who needs a drink to function? But still, having something right now to take the edge off is a good idea.

After pouring myself a glass of wine, I wander into the living room. Normally I'd make myself a plate of cheese and crackers to enjoy on the porch. I like sitting and letting the day wind down to a close while feeling the breeze on my face.

But not today. Today I walk around the living room, yanking the cord on each set of blinds. They all snap closed with a satisfying sound, and in a moment I'm completely shut off from the outside world. That's not my main goal, though, and I have to remember that.

I don't want to shut myself off from the rest of the world. I *like* the rest of the world.

I want to make sure nobody is going to be able to see me. The thought of someone peering through the slats in my blinds gives me chills. Before I can push that thought away, it takes hold, and I'm up, hurrying around the house, my glass of wine forgotten, as I yank all of the blinds shut.

Night is a long way off, but I'll sit inside until it comes. It hits me that I should go check the mail, and I hurry to the window, lifting a slat in the blind a fraction so I can look out.

Nothing moves outside. Even though I know I'm being ridiculous, I decide to stay right where I am.

It'll keep me from feeling like someone is watching me, at least.

17

COLLETTE

Wednesday morning I'm back at the library for my shift. Thanks to grief group right after work, I'll be heading out of here early, so I decided to come in early, not so I could work on repairing any books that needed extra love, but so I could look into the person Courtney has become.

First I navigate to the hospital's website and look her up. According to the write-up about her, she's highly educated and great at her job. She moved here a few years ago.

My stomach clenches when I think about what my life would have been like if she hadn't ever moved here. I'd still have my sister around, and I wouldn't be crouched over a computer in the back room of the library, looking up her murderer.

Still, I can't change the past. That's something Carol has finally gotten into my head after months of therapy. I can't change the past, but I can do something about how the future pans out.

There isn't much else to find out about her online. Thanks to a few well-photographed hospital functions, I'm able to see what she looks like and really study her face without worrying about getting caught or her realizing that I bear some resemblance to my sister. Her eyes are the same as they were before. She's gained some weight, so her cheeks are fuller, but she carries the weight well.

It's her.

My throat is tight as I close the tab so I don't have to keep looking at her. My next stop is the GIS for our county. Thanks to the records kept on all the homes and properties in the area, I can quickly look her up. The Geographic Information System gives me more information than I thought it would.

How much she paid for her house. How many acres it's on, and how many square feet it occupies. I know the exact size and shape of her deck and when she bought the house. Of course, the most important thing I find is one I write down on a scrap of paper that I then shove into my pocket for safe-keeping.

Her address.

By the time I make it to grief group, I'm so excited to talk to Jackson that I show up early and hang out in the parking lot. Gavin walks in, turning to speak to me as he passes, but I angle my body away, hopefully making it clear that I have nothing to say to him. Vince and Linda walk by, so deep in conversation that I only receive a wave from Linda.

That's fine. I want to talk to Jackson and tell him what I've learned.

A cold wind blows through, bringing with it the smell from the fried fish restaurant across the street. When I glance down at my watch, I'm surprised to see how quickly time is passing. He needs to show up soon, or he's going to be late, and Vince told me on my first day here that he'd lock us out if we were.

Was he joking? I have no idea, but I don't want to find out.

Scanning the parking lot, I check my watch, then shift my

weight back and forth. There's no good way to handle this. I want to talk to Jackson without anyone else around, but I don't want to be late to group.

The sound of a door opening behind me makes me turn to look. "Collette, we don't want to miss you." Vince smiles at me. "Is everything okay?" He glances down at my hand, and I know he's looking to see if I'm smoking.

"I'm looking for Jackson," I tell him, forcing a smile.

"Well, he'll be here if he wants to. You need to come on in, though. I don't want you to be late."

"Right." Still, I look once more out at the parking lot, hoping against hope that I'll see Jackson pull in. Nothing. No moving vehicles, nobody walking. Looks like I can stand out here like an idiot and hope he'll make it, or I can go on in where I'm supposed to be and play by the rules.

I decide to play by the rules.

Linda has saved my usual seat next to her, and I sink into it, trying to look grateful when I give her a smile. Across the circle from me is Jackson's empty seat, and I stare at it, willing him to suddenly appear. It's silly, and I know it, but I could really use a friend right now, and he's the closest thing I have to one.

Group passes quickly, uneventfully. I speak when I have to and nod at what I hope is the right time, but besides that, I mostly zone out. When I went online this morning to look up the good doctor, I didn't really expect to find anything useful.

Until I remembered how easy it is to find someone's address. It's disconcerting, really, the amount of information you can find out about someone online with a quick search. While there are some counties in the US that don't have all of this personal information so easily available, I'm lucky to live in one that does.

Without it, I'd have to head down to the courthouse and

ask the clerk there to look everything up for me. That would leave a trail, but thanks to the internet, I don't have one.

Right? Did I delete my history? I'd been so excited to find her address that I'm not sure if I took time to do that or not. Fear causes goosebumps to break out on my arms, and I rub my hands on my skin to warm back up.

"You cold? You can have my jacket." Linda leans over and whispers the words so we don't interrupt Gavin talking.

I shake my head. I'm freezing, but not because of the AC that seems to be permanently stuck on high in this room. It's like they're trying to freeze the grief out of us. If that actually worked, everyone would move to Antarctica, and all the therapists in the world would be out of business.

The only thing that's going to make me feel better right now is going back to the library and checking to make sure I deleted my history. I really don't think I did, don't think I remembered —

The sound of scraping chairs makes me snap out of my thoughts. Group is over; people are standing up. Vince stares at me, and I can tell before he says a word that he's going to come over and make sure I'm okay. Standing, I grab my purse, hold it like a shield, and prepare myself.

Everyone else is beelining for the snacks, but Vince hurries over to me, stopping me before I can join them. I take a step back, the backs of my knees whacking into the chair as I put some space between us.

"Collette, are you okay? You didn't seem yourself during group." There's concern written on his face, clear as day. Part of me feels bad that I was so zoned out, but I have a lot on my mind.

"I'm fine. Thanks for asking, I've been busy with work, and I think I'm really tired."

"You work at the library, right?"

I nod, wondering where he's going with this.

"When I was young, the library was my special place to go when I was stressed or needed a break. Never in my life did I think it would be a tiring place to work."

"Well, you know." I'm grasping as I try to think of what to say in response. I settle on parroting something Carol told me a while ago. "Anytime you deal with the public, you're going to run into stressful situations. It's the way it is."

"Sure. As long as you're okay, then I won't worry, but I know how quickly our grief can overtake us. If you're struggling and need help, then I need to make sure you're going to be willing to ask."

"Oh, Vince." It hits me what he's really asking. Under all his bluster and confidence, I suddenly realize that Vince is worried, not merely about me, but whether or not he's doing a good job taking care of me and providing me with the help I need. "I'm fine, really. Feeling tired and maybe overwhelmed." I pause, gauging his reaction before I continue. "Do you happen to know what happened to Jackson today?"

"If you're asking if he called ahead to tell me he wasn't going to be here, the answer is no. I don't know where he is or what he could have gotten into, but hopefully he's okay." A pause and he taps his chin with his finger while he looks at me. "But he knows the rules, as does everyone else here. If you're not on time, then you're not coming in."

"Right. You have your rules, and they keep this place running."

"Exactly. Now, if you'll excuse me, I could use some coffee. Don't hesitate to reach out if you need me, okay? Collette, grief is a wild animal. You need to remember that. You need to be careful of it, be wary, acknowledge that it exists, but make sure you don't fall prey to it. It can be a very slippery slope if you're not careful."

Don't I know it. "I'm fine, Vince. I'll see you next week, okay?"

"Right." He pats me on the shoulder like he's a distant father not quite sure how to connect with his child. "Okay then. Until next week, Collette, unless you need me, then you have my number."

"I do." I pat my purse to show him that I have it safely stored away. All of us in group have his card with his cell number printed on it. The promise is that if we need him, all we have to do is reach out and he'll be there for us. It's on us to reach out.

There's no way in hell I'm ever calling him.

18

COLLETTE

I connect my phone to Bluetooth and listen as the sound of ringing fills my car. "Pick up," I mutter, slowly reversing out of my parking space. Everyone else from group is still inside enjoying a donut and coffee, but the last thing I want is to stand around talking to everyone in there when there's really only one person I want to talk to.

"Collette." Jackson's voice wraps around me like a scarf, and I feel my entire body relax. Honestly, I hadn't noticed how tight my shoulders were or how stressed out I was feeling, but now that I'm finally talking to him, I can feel the tension draining out of me. "Is everything okay?"

"I wanted to ask you the same thing. Why weren't you at group?" I don't mean for my tone to be accusatory, but I immediately sense that it's come across that way anyway. "Are you okay?"

"Well, I would've been had I shown up to group on time, but I was a few minutes late, and the door was locked."

"I wondered if that was the problem." I pause, wanting to see him and talk to him but not wanting to come across too forward. It's a fine line, and I don't know that we're friends enough yet for what I'm going to ask, but I steel myself to do it.

"Do you want to grab a coffee?"

He says it first, the exact words I was going to ask him, like he was reading my mind.

"God, yes. I couldn't take one sip of that instant Folgers crap in a Styrofoam cup tonight. Where are you?"

"Downtown at Java Chip. Why don't you head this way, and I'll order you something."

"Sounds great. As big a cup as they make it, black. I'll pay you back when I get there."

"Please. I can afford coffee for a friend. See you soon." He hangs up.

I sit in the silence for a moment. Everyone else in grief group is still inside the room, but I'm off to spend time with my friend.

It's been a long time since I've had one of those. Sure, I have coworkers I like to talk to during lunch, but I'd never ask one of them to join me for coffee. I don't know why, but it seems like work and friendship need to be kept separate. But maybe something really good can come out of grief group besides the obvious improvements I should make while working through how much I miss Arabella.

I think what Carol and Vince don't realize is that part of how I feel about her and why I miss her so badly is because the woman who killed her is still out there. If she were dead... well, that's a horrible thing to articulate, but if she were dead, then maybe I could have some closure.

The road to Java Chip is mostly empty, and I tear through town, lucking out and finding a parking space right in front of the coffee shop. My car may not be the nicest on the road, and it certainly isn't the fastest, but it hasn't broken down yet.

The bright red color doesn't help it blend in much, but that's never really been a problem.

Well, not until I started following Courtney. *Amanda.* Whatever she wants to call herself.

As I walk through the parking lot, I scan the window, pleased to see Jackson sitting there watching me. He gives me a wave, and I wave back.

A friend. Not only that, but a friend who understands how hard it is to love someone and then lose them. Not many people can relate to the grief I feel when I think about Arabella. That, or they don't want to. They don't want to feel how painful it is when you allow yourself to miss someone you've lost.

The smell of coffee hits me as I open the door, and I hurry over to join Jackson. Like he promised, there's an oversized cup of black coffee sitting at the seat next to him, and I take a long swallow before pulling out a stool and sitting down next to him.

"Did I miss anything good at group?" He grins at me over what looks like a latte.

Briefly I wonder how long he's been here since the foam is almost to the top of his cup, and it doesn't look like he's had anything to drink from it yet, but maybe I drove faster through town than I realized.

"Nothing really. Everyone was there, but there weren't any big breakthroughs."

That's something I keep waiting to see. A breakthrough. According to Vince, any one of us can have a life-changing breakthrough at any moment. We're all ripe for it, and he's there to help guide us and hopefully make sure we can handle whatever the breakthrough entails. I haven't seen one in person yet, but I'm dying to. The way Vince describes it, it's almost a holy experience, and I'd love to witness one of those.

"Shame. And how are you feeling after your trip to see Courtney at the hospital?"

I'd almost forgotten that I told him what I was doing. In hindsight, it was probably a very stupid thing to do. Going to the hospital and pretending to be a patient who needed medical care was dumb, but I had to find a way to be closer to her.

I pause, gathering my thoughts and trying to decide what I'm going to say to him. This is where I want to be careful and not totally destroy the friendship the two of us are creating. "It was strange meeting her," I tell him. "But it's her, I know it is. I had to see her up close and personal to know for sure, but now there isn't any doubt."

"You're sure?" He puts his cup down and leans forward like he can't wait to hear what I'm going to say.

There's a radio playing music from the early 2000s, and I close my eyes for a moment, remembering what it felt like to be young and alive and to believe that nobody was ever going to take that from you.

"Collette?"

"Sorry, yeah. Zoned out for a moment. I'm sure. It's obvious now that I've met her."

He raises an eyebrow and slowly takes a sip of his latte before nodding for me to continue.

"I can see it in her eyes. She changed her name, changed her hair, but I'd know her anywhere." Tears sting my eyes, but I refuse to wipe them away. Nothing's worse than causing a scene.

"Did you say anything to her? Does she know that you know?"

I shake my head. Take a sip. Then another. "No, I was careful. But how am I going to stop her?"

"Stop her?" His voice is kind. "What do you want her to stop?"

Living. But I shrug instead of responding.

"Have you told Vince? Or anyone else in the group?"

"No. Do you think I should?" I hadn't thought about that. They're not my friends, not like Jackson is, but that doesn't mean they won't have something to add to the conversation. They might have some good ideas as to how I should handle things. Excitement runs through me when I think of what it would be like to have more than one person on my side.

"I think you need to be careful." Jackson brings me back down to earth with one sentence. "I don't want to be paranoid, Collette, but it sounds far-fetched."

"But you believe me, right?"

He nods and reaches out, taking my hand for a moment. Just one moment, just one squeeze, but in that single touch he tells me everything I need to know. "I believe you. I don't want the group to talk about you. I don't want them to think you..." His voice trails off.

"You don't want them to think I'm crazy?" I finish his sentence for him even though I don't like the way the words feel in my mouth.

He nods.

"But you don't think I'm crazy, do you?"

"Not at all." Again he squeezes my hand, then puts his back in his lap, waiting for me to speak.

"Okay, good." I exhale in relief. "If you don't think I'm crazy and I don't think I'm crazy, then the chances are pretty good that I'm not, right?"

"Absolutely." He's laughing, but so am I, so I don't feel at all strange about it. It feels good, honestly, to be sitting in a coffee shop with someone who has heard me talk about how badly I miss my sister and who obviously wants to help me through it. "So what's your plan? What are you going to do?"

"I could watch her?" I'm throwing it out there, testing the

waters. He doesn't know I followed her to the cemetery, and I'm not keen on telling him right now.

"You could." He takes a drink of his latte, and when he speaks again, I can smell the coffee on his breath. "You can do that, but you need to be careful that nobody accuses you of stalking her or anything like that. Are you sure you don't want to go to the police?"

"Not a chance. They won't believe me, and I don't want to go down that path. She's Courtney, and I have to prove it."

"Do you?" He must see the questioning look on my face, because he continues, "Have to prove it. Or will that be too difficult?"

I pause. I have a hangnail, and what I want to do right now is chew it off, but I fold my hands and put them in my lap, giving him all of my attention. There are some moments in your life that, after they happen, you will look back on them and realize how important and pivotal they really were. I don't have to look back on this moment to know that it's going to change my life and that I need to pay attention to what happens next.

"Jackson, I want you to listen to me and not judge, okay?"

He nods. When was the last time someone looked at me like this, like I have all of their attention and they're taking me seriously? It feels good.

"I'm going to follow her. I'm going to learn as much as possible about her. She has this amazing life that she's built after killing Arabella, and I want to take that from her."

He sucks his teeth. "You have to make sure —"

"I know it's her."

"That wasn't what I was going to say, Collette. I was going to tell you that you have to make sure you're careful. Grief is maddening; it's all-consuming. It can make it impossible for you to think straight."

He keeps talking, and I know I should listen to him. We're *friends*, after all, but I zone out for a minute.

I'm careful. I'm incredibly careful. After she lost me on Main Street and I couldn't catch up with her, after I barely saw her leaving the hospital yesterday and followed her to the cemetery, I know how careful I have to be.

I've got this.

I'm good.

19

AMANDA

It's always when you think that things can't become any worse that they start to bottom out. After feeling so foolish locked in my house on Tuesday and after being creeped out at the cemetery visiting Greta's grave, I knew I had to do something to stop feeling like this.

There's absolutely no reason for me to be afraid in my own home. There's also no reason for me to feel like I can't go to the cemetery without someone there with me. I've never felt nervous walking around downtown at night, never once stayed late in the library during medical school and been fearful that someone was going to hurt me.

The problem is this stupid red car. Even though I know it has to be a coincidence, I still have to remind myself of that when I'm out driving and see one. If I were a psychiatrist, I'd tell myself that I need exposure therapy so I could get used to the red cars without seeing them as a threat.

But I'm not. I'm much handier with a scalpel, but there's no way to incise the cars from my life. That's the thought that's on my mind when I walk into my office and find Brody

Whittaker, the CEO of the hospital, sitting at my desk waiting on me.

He's not across my desk, where I would have someone sit when they came to visit me to talk, but in my leather chair, his head leaned back a little, his eyes partially closed, like he wasn't able to keep them open.

"Brody?" I hate that my first reaction is fear. Not that he might be dead, although he certainly looks like he might, with how his eyes are mere slits and he's breathing so slowly he might as well not be breathing at all, but that something must be wrong.

"Oh, Amanda. Yes." My chair squeaks under his bulk as he sits up; then he gestures to a chair across from him. "Please, won't you join me?"

The fear becomes stronger as I lower myself into a chair, my eyes scanning my desk, looking for any sign of what he might be doing in here. When I got this job, he made sure to tell me that he wouldn't bother me, wouldn't come around needing things, unless something out of the ordinary was going on.

There's a mug of coffee where I usually put mine, and he takes a long sip of it, looking at me over the rim as he does.

I shift in my seat. This thing really isn't very comfortable. I should consider upgrading for my guests. "Is everything okay?"

"Amanda, do you know what day it is?"

"Friday." I'm relieved he's lobbing me an easy one to start with, although part of me is insulted. Of course I know what day it is. What game is he playing?

"Friday. Friday morning, early enough that I still need to mainline coffee to survive, and I'm in your office. I bet you can't figure out why."

I hate tricks. Slowly, I shake my head.

He exhales. "Because the hospital received a complaint."

A complaint? I sit up straighter in my chair now, the discomfort be damned. "What are you talking about?"

"A patient. Wrote a complaint. About you." He's doling out the words and watching me intently like he's going to be able to tell from the expression on my face exactly what happened.

I keep my face neutral, flat. On the inside I'm screaming, and I feel my fingers sink into the chair arms, but I don't want him to know how upset I really am.

"Do you know what it might be about?"

"No," I tell him, my voice as neutral as my expression.

"Well, would you like me to tell you?"

I nod. What choice do I have? Brody knows that he's not only in complete control, but that I have to play his game. That's why he ambushed me in my office this morning; that's why he decided to lie back in my chair; that's why he has his coffee sitting right in the middle of my desk.

If this were a big-dick contest, Brody would be winning, but that's only because I didn't know I needed to come to work ready to compete.

"A new patient." Pulling his phone from his pocket, he swipes it on, then glances at the screen before looking at me and shaking his head. "A new patient came to see you, terrified. She'd received a diagnosis and was told you were the best."

I am the best. I have to fight to keep from interrupting him. It won't do any good. He's the type of man who needs to hear himself talk, and the only thing I can do right now is be quiet and let it happen.

"So, of course, she wanted to see you. She did and thought everything was fine, but it turns out you were highly unprofessional."

I still don't say anything. It's only when he lowers his gaze at me over his phone that I realize he's waiting on me to defend myself.

"Does she give any examples or proof of how I was unprofessional?"

His eyes flick back to his phone. "'Not only did she cut me off, but she refused to treat me. She asked me to call my referring doctor to find out if I really needed treatment, to see if I had to come here. She was cold, unfriendly, and uncaring. Most of the hospital staff is a credit to the organization, but not Dr. Morgan. I'll never set foot in Mercy Heart again.'"

I'm racking my brain. Yes, it's been an incredibly long week, and yes, I might have had a few glasses of wine last night to help me pass out even though I was already exhausted, but there's only one patient who sticks out in my mind.

"I know who it was," I tell him, but he's not impressed.

"Who it was doesn't matter. Is it true you were this unkind to a woman with cancer? Is it true you asked her to call her primary care doctor herself instead of taking responsibility and doing it yourself?"

"I told her I was going to, but if she could follow up as well, then her doctor's office might send the documents and paperwork we needed faster. I —"

He holds up his hand, cutting me off. The expression on his face is that of a man who's finally putting a woman in her place, and he couldn't be happier about it. There have always been rumors that Brody went into hospital administration because he couldn't hack it in medical school, but I'd never believed them. Judging from the look in his eye right now, though, I do.

Oh, I do.

"You need to issue her an apology. This," he says, waving his phone at me like I'm going to be able to read the words on the screen, "is exactly the kind of reputation for a lack of consistent quality in our staff that we don't want. How are you going to fix this?"

Fix this? There are disgruntled patients every single day. Just because one of them happened to land in my office without her chart from her doctor isn't my problem.

Well, it shouldn't be. But the expression on Brody's face tells me that this is not only my problem, but that he's also going to be my problem until I figure out what to do about it.

"I will write her an apology," I grit out. "But first let me tell you my side. Or do you not want to listen to your doctors?"

His jaw tightens.

I continue, "She showed up here pretty concerned about what she was facing, without her chart being sent over from her primary care doctor. Normally I wouldn't even see a patient without all of that, but you know me, I'm a softie. The front desk got her in, promising to bill her insurance after everything was sent over. I met with her, told her I'd be happy to talk to her but that I couldn't give her specifics to her treatment without seeing her chart and without performing some diagnostics of my own."

He doesn't interrupt, and I take that as a good sign.

"The only thing I'm guilty of right now is trying to take care of a patient who came to my office without the necessary paperwork, being kind to a woman in distress, and doing everything possible to make her feel like she wasn't alone in the process. I have no idea why she would file a complaint against me, but you have to see that it's egregious."

"What I see is that you didn't act appropriately, didn't follow protocol, and saw a patient well before you were able to help her in any way. Issue an apology. And understand, Amanda, that this puts you on thin ice."

Thin ice? I've saved the lives of more patients than this man with his admin skills could ever imagine.

But I hold my tongue.

He stands up, putting his phone in his pocket, then braces his hands on my desk as he looks at me.

I stand, too, glad I wore heels this morning, glad I can tower over the man.

"Fix this. It goes on your record. Don't make me call a disciplinary meeting with you and HR." Then he's gone, moving from my office slowly, like he wants to take his time in my space. He doesn't look over his shoulder; instead he leaves the door wide open as he walks down the hall.

I feel like I can't breathe. Until recently my office has always been my safe space, especially after the panic and fear I felt this week when I was at home. How dare Brody come into it and throw his weight around over a stupid, baseless, nonexistent complaint? How dare he think he can bully me into doing something I don't want — and shouldn't need — to do?

Throwing myself into my chair, I grab paper and a pen. My heart slams so hard in my chest that I feel like I ran a marathon. I scrawl out an apology note on a pad of paper, then rip it up.

Can't call the patient *that* and expect to keep my job.

I'm fuming and need to be in a better headspace for the rest of the day, but I'm honestly not sure how to do that. All I know is that if I ever see Ms. Smith again, I'm going to let her have it for what she did to me. Why she'd throw me under the bus like that when I didn't do anything to her except show her some human kindness is beyond me, but now I have to fix it or end up in even more trouble.

20

COLLETTE

Friday morning I wake up, full of energy, and dress quickly for my job. My breakfast is a smoothie, maybe not the breakfast of champions we all want it to be, and it definitely won't hold me over to lunch, but I have a snack already packed. I feel giddy, like a kid on the first day of school, and I'm out the door well before I need to be, pulling into the library parking lot before anyone else is there.

Letting myself in and turning off the alarm, I slowly walk through the stacks as I switch on all the lights. It's magical, the way this place glows when it's woken up in the morning. I feel like a fairy or some kind of otherworldly creature waking everything up, dancing my fingers along the book spines, bringing the place to life.

There are a million stories in here, something for everyone. All my life I knew I wanted to work at a library. I can't write to save my life, but I can enjoy other people's stories. I can talk about them, share them, and love them. There are a dozen half-finished manuscripts on my computer, most of them hovering close to the trash.

I might not be able to write a compelling book, might not be able to bring people to tears or laughter or wisdom with my words, but there is one thing I can write.

I'm not only giddy because of the joy I feel when I'm in the library on my own, but also because of the complaint I sent to the hospital yesterday. It felt surreal writing it, knowing that the words I was putting down on paper would have the power to ruin someone else's day, if not their life, and I loved every single second of it.

It was easy to find the *contact us* page on the hospital website, easier still to write out my grievances. I put myself in the imaginary Ms. Smith's shoes, trying to see what it would feel like to not receive the care I so desperately needed during my first appointment. Sure, Dr. Morgan was amazing. She was kind and considerate. If I were really sick, then I would want her to take care of me.

But I'm not really sick, and she's not really Dr. Morgan. She's lying, so I feel like I have every right to lie too. If she would tell the truth about who she really is and what she's done to me, then I would be more than happy to come clean about my little lie. But as it is, we're in a stalemate.

Except I have a trump card, and I played it. Even though I don't have any idea where my complaint zipped off to through the internet when I pushed *send*, I have a very good feeling that a hospital with a reputation like Mercy Heart isn't going to ignore complaints like mine.

I felt like she didn't care. I felt like she wasted my time. I was scared and needed someone to look out for me, and she wasn't that person.

It was all a lie, but so is Ms. Smith. And so is Dr. Morgan.

As I clicked the send button, I had a momentary flash of panic that someone at the hospital might be able to find me, but that's not going to happen. I didn't leave any identifying information. Thanks to some Photoshop tutorials, I figured out how to make a pretty convincing fake ID and then printed it off, telling the front desk that I'd lost mine and this was a copy of it I'd kept at home in my safe.

Better to be prepared than in hot water.

They believed me.

Mercy Heart has Ms. Smith on record as coming in, but there's no way anyone would ever be able to tie her to me. I can't imagine that the two blondes in the nurses' station outside Dr. Morgan's office would be able to identify me. They didn't even realize that the person bringing them cookies and the cancer patient were the same woman.

"Idiots," I mumble, putting my purse in the small cubby where I stick my things during the day. I wish there were a way for me to check up on my complaint, but I didn't leave my phone number, so all I can do is hope that Amanda's having a rough morning. The thought of her being called to HR, sitting in a sterile office, listening to how terrible a person she is…it fills me with joy.

Slipping off my jacket, I tuck it into my cubby with my purse as my phone rings.

I freeze.

Who in the world would be calling me this early? I guess it could be Sara, letting me know she's having car problems or isn't going to make it to the office, so I pick up the phone without really thinking about it.

"Hello?" I'm loud, confident. Even though I don't recognize the number, it could still be Sara. She could have borrowed someone else's phone. Jackson could be calling me from his office. I'm alone in the library, and there's no reason why I shouldn't pick up the call to see what someone needs.

"Good morning, this is Dr. Morgan at Mercy Heart. Is this Blue Ridge Medical?"

The voice is bright, confident. It washes over me, and fear snakes up my spine. As happy as I was a moment ago, I now feel the complete opposite. It feels like I've been plunged into an ice bath, and I feel my fingers tighten on the phone. Swallow. Answer.

"This is; can I help you?"

How could I have forgotten that my Google number for the fake medical office I go to is directed to this phone? It was stupid of me to pick it up, stupid of me to make the number in the first place. I'd thought it would make this entire thing easier if I needed to call Mercy Heart and make sure I got an appointment.

"Oh, good, I wasn't sure if you'd be answering your phones this early."

I look at my watch. It's before eight, but not by much. I have to open the doors soon, and Sara will be here before then. Our volunteers and other staff will show up, everyone ready to put their things away in this back room and start the day, and I need to end this call.

Now.

"We're actually quite busy with patients. Can I put you on hold?" My finger hovers over the end call button. Why I don't push it, I don't know. I think I want to talk to this woman a little longer. I want to hear more from the woman who killed Arabella.

"No, I don't have the time for that, I'm sorry. I was calling to see if you could please send over Belle Smith's chart? I saw her and requested for it to be sent over but still don't have it. There's no way for me to begin her treatment without it."

My mind races. "We already sent it. Are you sure it was filed correctly?"

"You sent it?" She sounds genuinely confused.

I would feel sorry for her, but I don't. I like how she sounds rather more frazzled than she might like. Maybe I was right in my daydream. Maybe she's already been called in to talk to HR.

"Do you mind checking again?"

"Listen, Doctor," I say, propping one hand on my hip and grinning. I have the upper hand now, and it feels really, really good. "I'm sorry that you misplaced the file, but a mistake on your part doesn't constitute an emergency on mine. Now, if you'll excuse me, I have patients I need to help, and it sounds to me like you need to spend some time organizing your office."

Before she can respond, I hang up.

I'm glowing. Sweating. Whatever, maybe it's a combination of both. Whatever it is, I'm over the moon, absolutely overjoyed at the strain I heard in her voice. Amanda might think she's so smart because she got away with murder and is now a doctor, but she's not. All it took was a complaint and a Google phone number and I ruined her day.

The sound of laughter reaches me, and I hurriedly turn my phone off and slip it into my purse. I don't want to risk her calling back and one of the library volunteers thinking they're being helpful by picking up the call.

Volunteers. Using the computer. Maybe checking the history of what everyone has been looking at because only nosy people become volunteers so they can obtain insider information and gossip about staff without going through the trouble of getting a full-time job.

Oh, God. Did I delete my history? It's been logged since Wednesday, plenty of time for someone to see it. I forgot yesterday. I've been so distracted, thinking only of the doctor, thinking of Arabella.

Hurrying now, I rush to the computer and turn it on, drumming my fingers on the desk while it warms up. A moment later I'm online, clicking the history button so I can make sure I deleted my search for her address.

The laughter grows closer.

I should have done this first thing this morning, but I

wasn't thinking about it. My daydream about the good doctor getting in trouble distracted me.

The history tab opens, letting me see every website staff has visited. My palm is sweaty, but I don't dare let go of the mouse long enough to wipe my hand on my pants.

I hear footsteps right outside the room. Casting a glance at the door, I'm relieved to see I shut it behind me. That will keep whoever's out there out of my space for a moment longer while they unlock it.

There. My internet search for her address. I click the link, my heart in my throat, then delete it, working my way down the list to cover my tracks. There are a few links to delete, and I click each one, moving faster now, racing against time.

The door swings open.

I'm rushing now as I click out of the browser and turn off the monitor. My cheeks feel flushed. Spinning around, I slap a smile on my face.

Act natural.

Sara leads a small group of staff and employees into the room. She's got a giant grin on her face, a pan of warm cinnamon rolls in her hands, and she lights up even more when she sees me.

"Collette! I hope you're hungry. We only have a few minutes to eat before we have patrons coming in, but I was up early baking and thought everyone would enjoy a nice warm breakfast."

"You know what? I'm starving." I grab paper plates and plastic forks from the cupboard and put the stacks on the table for everyone to reach.

This day started out amazing. I don't know how it can possibly improve.

21

AMANDA

Normally on Saturday morning I'm drinking tea, watching the lawn crew work in my yard, and thinking about going to Tito's later for a bite to eat and a drink, but the only constant in my life right now is tea.

I'm on my third cup and still in my pajamas. Yesterday was easily the worst day I've ever had at work. It started out terribly with Brody sitting at my desk. I know he loved dropping the complaint bomb on me. That man hates me, I know he does. He hates any woman smarter than him.

Then, when I called the doctor's office to see where the chart was, I was told it had already been sent over. I have no reason to think they were lying to me, but also no chart. Either it got lost on the way to the hospital, which is unheard of, or someone is messing with me.

I think about the blondes as I take another sip of my Earl Grey. It's entirely possible that they have the chart and simply don't want to give it to me, but why would they do that? No, we don't always see eye-to-eye, and we did have that argument right before I saw Ms. Smith without her chart, but still.

Groaning, I drop my head into my hands. The worst part

of all of this is that it's my fault. I never should have seen a patient without a chart and all of their information. It was stupid of me to do that, to agree to let Ms. Smith into my office without everything I needed. I didn't want her to have to delay her care, and honestly, I thought the chart would be here by now.

"So who dropped the ball?" There isn't an answer, but it's not like I really expected one in the silence of my house. Turning my mug on the table, I listen to the scraping sound, my mind working overtime as I try to think about how to handle whatever comes next. I wrote the apology to Ms. Smith and emailed it to Brody since I didn't have any way to contact the patient.

The phone number she left for us to reach her was for a local butcher. The email we had on file bounced right back to my inbox. I don't know what's going on, but the fact that Brody thinks I'm in the wrong here is enough to drive me nuts. Something's off with the entire situation, but of course I'm going to be the one to take the fall.

And then it hits me. "I'm sure the front desk girls would have gotten a copy of her driver's license." Belle Smith may think she's a ghost, but she drove to her appointment, right? I guess she could have called an Uber or come with a friend, but this is my only shot to find out what this woman really wants with me.

Before I can second-guess myself and talk myself down off the ledge I'm currently standing on, I've changed my clothes and am in the car. Thanks to how many times I've driven to the hospital, I don't even have to think about the turns as I take them. The car moves like it's on autopilot, and it gives me plenty of time to think about what I'm going to do next.

Sure, it's strange for me to be in the hospital on a Satur-day. I only come in when I'm really worried about a patient and want to make sure they're doing okay after treatment or surgery, and I've never asked the front staff to pull a chart for me unless the patient is in the hospital, but there's no reason why I can't do that.

I have to hope nobody tries to question me.

My hands are sweaty as I walk up to the entrance, and I wipe them on my jeans before heading to records. This part of the hospital is quiet on the weekend. The emergency room is on the opposite side of the building, and there's where all the action is right now. I'm totally fine not seeing many people as I hurry down the hall.

It's quiet, but still it feels like I'm at work on a normal weekday. The intercom keeps buzzing and calling for various doctors to head to the ER. The same antiseptic smell burns my nose. I pass a few nurses giggling and holding onto each other as they walk, obviously caught in the laughing fit of some joke, probably told by an intern looking to lighten the mood.

The records desk is right in front of me, and I take a deep breath, trying to look as casual as possible. It's one thing to come down here for a chart I need for a current patient, another to come here because I think someone is trying to...

What?

What do I think she's trying to do? It was pretty obvious by the specificity of the complaint filed against me that it's Belle Smith who wasn't happy with her treatment, but why would she do that when I made it clear I would help her as soon as I received her file from her doctor's office?

And what, exactly, is her end game?

That's a question I can't answer, not without knowing more about her. As I walk up to the desk, my heels clicking on the floor, the receptionist looks up at me, her face brightening when she sees me.

"Dr. Morgan, what a surprise! You look very casual without your white coat on. I almost didn't recognize you."

Crap. I should have worn my white coat to appear more official walking around the hospital. Too late now, so I smile back, trying to sound relaxed.

"Thanks, Cindy." I have to glance at her name tag, but the effort is worth it. She's beaming now. "I actually wanted to check up on the details of a new patient. Her doctor's office was supposed to send over her chart, and I want to see if we have it yet."

It's not a lie. I'm sticking as close to the truth as possible, and that's what I think will help me get what I really want. When you lie, which you shouldn't anyway, you need to make sure you keep your lie close to the truth. The farther away from the truth you stray, the harder it is to remember what you've lied about and to keep your lies straight.

I want to check up on a patient and see if we have her chart. That's the truth. What I don't tell Cindy is that the patient is a liar, threw me under the bus, and I want to see where she lives.

"Oh, sure. Name?" Her fingers are poised to fly over her keyboard.

"Belle Smith."

"Like *Beauty and the Beast*?" She glances up at me while she searches.

I shrug.

"Yeah, probably from *Beauty and the Beast*, depending on her age. Alright, I see where her chart will be; hang on a second." She hops out of her chair so quickly she leaves it spinning behind her and returns a moment later with a file. "Looks really slim, Dr. Morgan. I don't think the chart got sent over."

I know it didn't.

"Not a problem, thanks." I reach for it, and she holds onto it a moment.

"You know I can't let you walk away with it."

"I'm only looking at it, Cindy." My smile feels forced. "I'll poke through it, see if everything is in order, find the information I need for her treatment, and then hand it right back." She still looks dubious as I almost tug it from her grasp. "Her *breast cancer* treatment," I say, lowering my voice so the words are for her ears only.

"Oh." Her mouth stays in a perfect O after she speaks. Rumors and insider information are currency in the hospital. Cindy could have guessed the patient was a cancer patient since she's mine, but now she knows more about her than other people do.

Turning my back on her desk, I lean against the counter and flip the folder open. It's as slim as it was the morning she came in to see me, and I grow frustrated. The paperwork has been filled out quickly, like Belle was in a hurry, scrawling her name on everything. Her chicken scratch rivals mine, and it takes me a minute to decipher it.

Twenty-two Old Horse Road. I whisper her address to myself to make sure I won't forget it, then flip the page, looking for a copy of her driver's license. We ask patients for these so we can verify their information.

There it is. Belle Smith of Old Horse Road. She's five feet three inches, which seems about right, with blonde hair and hazel eyes. Oh, and she's an organ donor, good for her.

There's only one problem, and I wouldn't even notice it if I weren't paying incredibly close attention.

Turning, I put the folder down on the counter and lift the photocopy of the driver's license.

"Everything okay?" Cindy looks up from her computer. By leaning forward a fraction, I can see that she's playing solitaire.

"It's all fine, don't worry." Still, I squint at the driver's license. Something about it doesn't seem right. It takes me another moment to figure it out, but when I do, I'm surprised it took me that long.

It's her name. Belle Smith, written there as clear as a bell, but after Smith there's a smudge, like something was there and then was deleted. I rub my finger over the paper. Nothing comes off.

Not deleted. Changed. "Hey, do you know if there are houses or apartments on Old Horse Road?"

Cindy looks up from her clicking. "Maybe? On the far end by the lake, right? I know they were talking about building some apartments there a few years ago, but I don't know if they ever actually did it."

"Thanks." One small smudge on the driver's license doesn't mean anything, but combined with the strange address, it could mean something. Tapping the papers back into place in the file, I hand it back over Cindy's desk. "You have a great weekend, okay?"

"You got it. Bye, Dr. Morgan."

I turn before she can say anything else and yank my phone from my pocket. It takes a moment for my maps app to open and for me to type in Belle's address. As I'm walking down the hall, I run into some dead space, so the app doesn't respond until I'm already out of the building.

The heat is oppressive, even early this morning. It presses down on me, making me sweat. But when I look at my phone, chills run up my spine.

Overdone? Definitely.

True? Yes.

Because the address on Belle's driver's license pulls up as one for a meat market, not a home, not an apartment building. My finger trembles when I tap the phone icon to make the call.

"Billy's Butcher, can I help you?" A pause. "Hello? Is anyone there?"

I hang up. Pressing my hands firmly on my thighs, I lean over and take some deep breaths, trying to calm down.

This means nothing. Maybe the butcher moved and the address hasn't updated online.

But I'm kidding myself. I know I am.

22

COLLETTE

Jackson meets me at the donut table, waiting until I've moved out of the way a little bit so he can grab something to eat. I watch him as he pours us each a coffee, grab mine from the table, and step away from everyone else so we can talk. The weather outside is terrible, a crazy thunderstorm that swept in earlier this afternoon. If I hadn't promised Carol I'd come to group and if I didn't want to talk to Jackson, I might have skipped tonight.

But we have a lot to talk about.

"So how have you been?" His question is casual, lobbed like a tennis ball over the net, something easy for me to hit back. "You staying safe?"

The implication is clear. *Are you keeping out of trouble while stalking your sister's killer?*

"Of course I am." I take a sip of coffee. It's as terrible as it is every other Wednesday, but right now I don't care. I take another sip before speaking again. "I reported her to the hospital."

Linda walks by us, and I press my lips together, trying to hold back a laugh while Jackson stares at me. His mouth drops open like he can't quite believe what he heard; then he gives his head a shake.

"You *what*?"

"Reported her. I don't know if anything will come of it, but I can't imagine she'll be thrilled about it. I want her to know that someone knows what kind of person she really is."

"And did you hear anything back? Sometimes when you file a complaint, the company will call you back, let you know how they handled it, that sort of thing."

"Nope." I pop the *P*. "I didn't leave my phone number, and the address I gave them is fake. There's literally no way she could find me, Jackson."

"Oh, Collette." He runs his hand through his hair and exhales hard. "I know you want to hurt her, but are you sure this is the best option right now? Don't you think you should be gathering proof?"

There's a ticking bomb in my chest. I have to take some deep breaths to prevent it from going off. "I *do* have proof, Jackson. You and I have been over this time and time again, and it's honestly getting old. What would you have me do? You know I won't go to the police; that's a nonstarter. So if you have a problem with how I'm handling things, then —" I cut myself off and turn away, wanting nothing more than to leave.

The only proof I have about Courtney is sister's intuition, and that's not exactly something that will hold up in court. I don't need to explain to Jackson *why* I know that Courtney is still alive. He needs to trust me.

He was so supportive, but as soon as I start taking action against her, he gets cold feet? What is that about? Why would he suddenly turn his back on me? I'm not entirely sure, but I do know I'm not interested in standing around here and having him act like he's a better person than I am.

"Collette, wait." He grabs my arm, and I still, letting him slowly turn me back around.

I can talk a big game to myself about how I don't need him, but Jackson is my best friend. I want him to be on my side, and I want to be able to talk to him about the things I'm finding out. If I don't have him to talk to, then I'm only going to be talking to myself.

"Okay, hear me out." He lowers his voice some more, looking around the room to make sure nobody is paying attention to us. "I know you don't want to talk to the police, and I respect that." I open my mouth to complain, but he holds up a finger to stop me. "How about this? You said you have proof. You said you have all the information you need to expose her, right? Why don't you involve the news?"

"The news?"

"Yeah, the news. Don't act so incredulous. I know you got the short end of the stick with Arabella's death, and you don't trust the police, but there's no reason to think that the press wouldn't help you now. You've been doing so much, looking into Arabella's death and her killer, and now maybe it's time to let someone with a few more resources help you out."

"I already found out where she lives."

He stares at me for a moment. "I want you to be safe, okay? I care about you. Take a night off and reach out to the papers. Let them do some of the legwork for you. Who knows, you might crack the whole thing open with their help, and then you can finally find the peace that you deserve."

"It's not for me. It's for Arabella," I say, but my mind is already working overtime as I think about what he suggested. There's no reason to believe it wouldn't work, no reason to think that a journalist couldn't help me. Jackson is right. I've done all of the legwork this far, and all I need to do is hand the reins over to someone else.

"Are you thinking about a sit-down with a journalist?" I'm picturing myself on *Good Morning America*, exposing all of the lies that surround what happened to my sister. "This could be huge."

"Let's start smaller," he tells me, and even though I know he's only trying to temper my expectations so I don't end up disappointed, I can't help that it hurts. "I have no idea how big this thing could go, but if you have all the proof you're saying you do, then any good paper will take the story and run with it."

"How do I do that?"

"Oh, that's easy." He grins at me, and I feel the knots in my stomach unclench. "I'm surprised more people don't do this when they're really upset by something, because it's a great way to get someone's attention when you need to bring a problem to light."

Under an hour later I'm sitting at home in my pajamas, my computer screen casting a glow on my face. I feel warm, excited. Hope courses through me, and I lace my fingers together, cracking them away from my body before resting them on the keys.

Jackson's idea had been a letter to the editor. At first I hadn't been so sure. How many letters to the editor have we all read where the person comes across either totally unhinged or like all of their problems could be solved by them having a nice glass of wine? But I'm different, and I have to keep reminding myself of that.

I have a real problem.

My fingers fly across the keys, and after a while I sit back, pleased. I've read it half a dozen times now, and I hit the print button. Next to me, my ancient printer groans as it slowly spits out the page.

Sure, I could email it in, but my internet here is patchy at best, especially in a terrible storm, and I'll drop it by the paper's office in the morning. I don't even need to stay to see what anyone says, because I'll be able to read the letter in print in a few days.

Snatching the paper from the tray, I take it into the kitchen and put it on the counter by my purse. Even though I'm not really tired yet, I still head to bed.

Tomorrow is going to be an amazing day.

23

COLLETTE

I don't think I've gotten the paper delivered to my house since I was little and living with my parents. My dad lived for the morning paper and read it every day at breakfast, spreading the pages out on the table like they were the scripture. He didn't merely read the paper — he absorbed it. He was like a sponge, taking in all of the information he possibly could and then talking about it until the news moved on to something else.

It didn't matter what it was, the top news story became his fodder for the next twenty-four hours. From a new school building being put up across town to a shooting, to industrial accidents, to a retirement notice, my dad read it all. He also loved the letters to the editor and would read them aloud to Arabella and me, pausing dramatically, wiggling his eyebrows at the good parts, making sure we were paying attention.

And then he would quiz us. It was like it wasn't enough for him to tell us about the news. He wanted us to remember it, to marinate in it the way he did, then be able to discuss it at dinner.

After he died, my mom stopped the paper. She gathered up all the pages he'd strewn about the house, all the clippings he'd gathered and carefully filed away to look at later, and put them in the recycling. The last time I cared about a newspaper was when the article about Courtney Barrow's supposed death was printed.

Thank God Mom wasn't alive when Arabella died.

But now I'm on my way downtown to buy myself a copy of the local paper. I dropped off my letter to the editor on Thursday and was told that if they decided to print it, it would appear by the weekend.

It wasn't in the paper yesterday morning, but now it's Saturday, and I can't help how excited I am. Everything I do the rest of the day hinges on whether or not my letter made it into print. I need to see if my letter is featured, if it's interesting enough for a reporter to pick it up and then want to look into it. Jackson had a great idea in skipping over the police entirely by involving the news instead, and now I need to know how well my plan worked.

It's dark out. I haven't even eaten breakfast before slipping behind the wheel and hurrying out. Henry was still curled up on the end of the bed when I left, only opening one angry amber eye to glare at me for interrupting his slumber before rolling over and passing back out.

Maybe I'll climb back into bed with him when I return home with the paper. Or maybe I'll want to celebrate.

Above me the full moon is so bright that it feels like it must be early morning, but the sun won't be up for a while yet. I'm alone on the sidewalk although I can smell that someone is already baking this morning. Probably the coffee shop, Java Chip. They like to pretend all of their baked goods are homemade, but I have it on good information from a library patron that everything is brought in frozen and raw, then baked.

Still, it smells good.

Feeding the quarters into the paper box takes time, and my hand trembles as I pull open the handle, taking the top paper from the stack. For a moment I debate buying two. Then I'd have one to cut out my letter and store it with my other clipping and an untouched paper to keep, but I can buy an additional copy later. Right now I want to hold it in my hands. I don't want to have to wait any longer.

I'm vibrating with excitement. It's one thing to hope that my words will be printed, another to see them in real life. Even though I want to hurry home for something to eat, I hurry over to a bench and sit, spreading the paper carefully on my lap. The weekend paper is always full of fun things to do around town, but I don't even glance at those articles as I flip the pages, looking for the letters to the editor.

It takes me a moment to find them. Some clouds blow across the sky and block out the moon. I end up pulling my phone from my pocket and using the flashlight to see the words on the page.

There's a sick feeling in my stomach when I think that maybe it wasn't printed. I don't know why I'm afraid, but, for a second, I can't see it.

Slowing down, I start at the beginning, prepared to read every single letter to the editor until I find mine, but I don't have to. I have no idea how I missed it the first time around, but there it is, right on top.

The first one.

No one will miss it. Not even Amanda.

24

AMANDA

Saturday morning dawns clear and bright, and I only wake up when the sun moves enough for a strip of light to land right on my face. Groaning, I sit up, then stretch, forgetting for a moment the week I've had.

Then everything that's been going on hits me, and I flop back down in my bed, grabbing a pillow and holding it over my mouth so I can scream.

It feels good.

Screw my normal Saturday routine. Today is different. I shower quickly and dress, then head downstairs, pausing long enough to open the blinds in the living room.

Slats of light shoot through the dark, and I press my eye up against one space. I can't shake the feeling that someone is watching me. Following me. I hate that I'm living like this, like I'm terrified of my own shadow. It's insane that someone like me, as educated and successful as I am, could be afraid of anything outside my house, but that's the truth of it all.

"You know what? No. I'm not going to live like this any longer." Stalking to my front door, I unlock it and throw it open. The screen door is still locked, but at least now I can have some light and fresh air in my house.

"It's not enough." Anger drives me as I unlock the screen door and open that, too, stepping out onto the porch to look around the neighborhood.

I step in something wet.

"Oh, ew," I say, lifting my bare foot and wiping it on the welcome mat behind me. "What in the world is that?"

It's mud. There's mud on my front porch, which shouldn't be a big deal, when you think about it. Mud belongs outside, so of course it would make it up onto my porch from time to time.

"Are those..." My voice trails off, and I squat down, getting closer to the mud so I can really look at it. "Footprints?"

They're unmistakable. I don't need to squat down like this to tell what they are except for the fact that it honestly seems so preposterous that I want a better look at them. Before I know what I'm doing, I reach out and lightly touch one. The mud transfers easily to my fingers, and I wipe it on my jeans as I stand back up.

And then the heavy reality of what this means hits me, and I take a step back into the doorway, my eyes flicking back and forth as I look around the neighborhood.

Someone was here last night. Someone walked around my house, treading into mud, then came and stood on my front porch. They didn't knock; they didn't ring the bell; they just *stood*.

No, that's wrong. When I look along the length of the front deck, I see footsteps along it. They disappear part of the way down, but only because they were growing lighter and lighter as the mud transferred onto my porch. But I can see where the person went, and I can see that they were looking in my windows.

Well, trying. My blinds were pulled, tight as shut eyes.

"Oh, God." I haven't eaten anything so far this morning, but that doesn't stop the sick feeling in my stomach, and I back the rest of the way into the house, slam the door and lock it, then run for the bathroom. I barely reach the toilet before I throw up.

"Oh, God," I repeat, wiping my hand across my mouth. "God, what in the hell is going on?"

My first thought is that I need to get out of here, but where would I go? If someone is watching me for whatever reason, then they're going to be able to follow me. No, my house is the safest place for me to be right now. There was someone trying to look in at me last night, but they weren't able to break in, and that's all that matters.

"I have to call the police." My phone is in my pocket, and I fumble it out, dialing 911 with shaking fingers. The dispatcher answers, and I sink down to sit on the cold tiles. "Someone was looking in my house," I tell her. "There are footprints on my front porch."

She's calm. Unflappable. I guess you have to be to do that job when you never know what kind of call you're going to answer next, what kind of terrible day someone is going to be having when they break down and reach out for help. She tells me to stay inside, to keep my phone near me. That someone will be here as soon as possible.

I hang up, leaning my hand back against the vanity. My eyes fall on the open bathroom door.

Someone could be in the house with me.

That fear drives me to my feet. Gasping, I lunge for the door, slamming it shut. The lock slips easily into place, and I turn my head, resting my ear against it.

Nothing. All I can hear is my heartbeat in my ear. I shift, pressing my ear against it again, but it's the same thing.

If someone is in my home, then they're being very sneaky.

Seven minutes pass, and I still stand like that. Unmoving. Terrified. Sweat runs down my lower back, and I exhale hard.

Never in my life have I felt fear like this. My fingers and toes are cold, almost numb. I feel my heart beating, but it's almost like the blood it's pumping is thick, a sludge through my veins. Every breath is loud, and I hold the air in my lungs, waiting before I exhale, waiting because I might miss the sound of someone moving in my house.

Then I hear them.

Sirens.

They're coming with sirens.

Without thinking, I reach for the doorknob, then stop.

They're not here yet. I can hear them, but they're not here. How do I know someone isn't right on the other side of the bathroom door, their ear pressed up against the wood, timing their breaths with mine? I can see them when I close my eyes. I see the expression on their face, how thrilled they are that I'm terrified.

Only a narrow sheet of wood separates us.

Revulsion forces me to push back from the door. I don't have anything in here that could be used for a weapon, but I still look around, hoping there will be a knife, a club, something I can use to protect myself.

Nothing. Shampoo. A dull razor I keep meaning to replace. Fluffy teal towels.

No weapons.

"Help me," I gasp out, even though there isn't anyone here to hear me.

I turn around, still desperate for something that will protect me; then I see it.

The window.

It's slim, but so am I. Positioned right above the toilet, it's designed to let air and light in but not be easily accessible by anyone inside or outside the home, but I have to try. I have to get out of here. As quietly as possible, I close the toilet lid. The sirens have stopped. The police are here. I'll do anything to escape the house and join them.

I have to tell them that I think someone is in the house. They'll clear it; they have weapons and armor. I won't have to worry about something happening to me because they'll keep me safe.

The latch turns smoothly, and I press up on the window, holding my breath until it silently slips into place.

Thank God it didn't groan.

Now comes the hard part.

I angle my body, turning so I can put one leg out the window, then sit straddling it as I push my head and arm through. The air outside is fresh and clean, nothing like the air I've been trapped in, and I gulp it down.

I don't even realize I'm crying until I taste the salt on my lips.

Halfway there.

All I have to do is hang onto the windowsill as I pull the rest of my body through the space, then turn and drop onto the waiting ground. It's easy.

"No big deal." I'm still whispering even though I want to scream.

From inside the house I hear the doorbell ring. The cops are there, right around the corner, ready to help me, and I'm dangling out the window like a crazy person.

"Help!" The scream rips from my throat before I realize it's me calling for help. "I'm around the side of the house; please help me!"

Almost out the window now. My other leg catches for a moment, but then I feel myself pop free from the house. I'm balanced, one knee on the windowsill, my hands cramping from hanging on for dear life. All I have to do is let my legs dangle and then drop.

Or I could jump. Turning to look over my shoulder, I attempt to gauge how far it is to the ground if I were to push back from the house and let gravity take over.

An officer runs around the corner of the house, his gun drawn.

"Oh, thank goodness," I say, holding out one hand to reach for him.

"Don't move! Keep your hands where I can see them!"

25

COLLETTE

"You want to know what I love, Henry?" I ask, scratching him under the chin as he works his way closer and closer to my breakfast. He wants a piece of bacon, but every time I think about relenting and giving him one, I imagine Arabella's voice in my mind fussing at me for trying to kill her cat. "I love morning rides on Saturdays. Do you want to come with me?"

He shoots me a disdainful look.

I shrug, standing and picking up my plate. There's one piece of bacon left, and I wave it in the air before popping it in my mouth.

That was probably a mistake. If cats could frown, that would be what he's doing right now, and I have a very good feeling he's going to throw up in my shoes later.

"Stay out of my closet," I tell him, but he's already jumped from the table and run out of the kitchen. "Little furry jerk. If Arabella hadn't loved you more than anything in the world, do you know what you'd be right now? A rug!" I raise my voice so he can hear me, but he's already disappeared to plot his revenge.

That's fine. We all deal with grief in different ways. We both want revenge. I want it on the woman who killed Arabella. He wants it on me for being part of why she's dead.

Sighing, I wash my plate and put it in the drying rack before grabbing my keys and purse. It feels dangerous to drive out past Amanda's house this morning, but I want to check on her. I was there last night, paying her a visit, and then downtown this morning picking up the paper.

It's time to go back and check on her, see if she realizes I swung by her house.

My muddy sneakers are in the bathroom after a good scrub-down, so I put on some flip-flops and head outside. Today is going to be gorgeous, and I wish I had a convertible so I could put the top down and let the wind whip through my hair. I don't, so instead I roll down all four windows on my way across town.

Someone like Amanda has probably never visited my crappy apartment complex. It's not exactly on the radar of anyone in town who has money, so I don't blame her, but I like getting out of here from time to time and seeing how the other half live. It's probably risky to keep going to her neighborhood, but I can't help myself.

I like cruising through, checking out the houses and the perfectly manicured lawns. I like seeing her neighbors, and I always wave to them.

They wave back.

I don't belong in her neighborhood, but I like pretending.

This morning, however, something is different. I can tell as soon as I pull onto her road. Instead of being met with the sound of lawn mowers as everyone competes for the nicest lawn in town, I'm met with flashing blue and red lights.

My hand moves automatically, turning down the music I was blasting on my way over here. There are three police cars parked in Amanda's driveway.

My stomach twists. I'm torn between wanting her to be okay and wanting her to be dead. I want her to suffer for what she did to Arabella, but I don't want her to have taken the easy way out.

I drive by slowly, doing my best not to look like I'm cruising through to see what's going on. Amanda isn't anywhere in sight, so she must be in the house. As I drive by, I see one officer on the front porch. He stands and presses his face against the window.

Exactly like I did last night.

Did she call about my muddy footprints? Laughter bubbles up in me, and I clamp a hand over my mouth to prevent the sound from escaping. Did I bother her that much that she ended up calling the police?

I reach the cul-de-sac at the end of the neighborhood and slowly drive around it. Now I'm almost nervous to head back past her house. What if she sees me drive by? What if she recognizes me from the appointment we had in her office? What if she tells the police that I was there for no good reason, and then I filed a complaint against her?

I stop the car.

What I need to do is keep driving and get the hell out of here. I need to put as much distance between Amanda and me as possible, but I feel like I can't take my foot off the brake. There's only one way in and out of this neighborhood, and I'm going to have to drive past her house to leave.

Slowly, like I can avoid what's going to happen, I take my foot off the brake. I'm about to gas it when a man appears in front of my car, clippers in his hand, a floppy straw hat on his head.

"Hey!"

I stiffen.

He waves. "Hey, can I help you?"

Shit. "No, I got lost," I tell him, leaning part of the way out the window. He takes my movement as an invitation and walks around to talk to me. "Sorry, I thought I knew where I was and then got turned around. You know how it is."

The expression on his face tells me that no, he does not know how it is. "Don't you have GPS?"

"Do what?" His question takes me completely by surprise. "Oh, yeah, but I wasn't using it."

"Where are you trying to go? Maybe I can help you." Reaching out, he rests his hand on my car. I can't help but think he's holding me here so I can't leave.

"Um, Timon Street?"

A frown. "I don't know that one."

Of course he doesn't. It's on my side of town, somewhere I doubt he's ever been. "I'm sorry to disturb the quiet here," I say, gesturing at the road ahead of me. "I'll be on my way. Maybe I'll even turn on my GPS."

He doesn't move his hand from my car. "You're not part of the reason why there are so many cops down the road, are you?"

Yes. "No."

"Hmm." He stares at me like he's memorizing my face. I shouldn't have come here. It's one thing to come at night when everyone is asleep, but another entirely to be so stupid as to come in the middle of the day.

"I'll be going. The yard looks great," I tell him, slowly inching forward. He has to take the hint. He has to let go of my car so I can leave.

My throat is tight. My palms are sweaty. If he could hear how fast my heart is hammering away in my chest, then there's no way he'd let me go right now. I know these places and how they are about neighborhood watch and looking out for everyone else. There's no doubt in my mind that everyone will know there was a suspicious person on the street as soon as I pull out of the neighborhood.

But all I can do is hope he won't call out to the police, won't draw their attention.

"Please," I choke out. "I can't be late for my appointment."

"On a Saturday?" He frowns. But he lifts his hand from my car.

"Thank you." Before he can change his mind or try to stop me, I press down on the gas, pulling away from him.

He doesn't move.

I watch him in my rearview mirror as I make a curve. He's still standing there, his clippers in his hand, an unreadable expression on his face.

Thank goodness. Now I need to leave this neighborhood before Amanda sees me. I'll come back. But only in the dark. Only when there's no chance I'll see her face-to-face.

Her house is on my left now, and I keep my eyes on the road as I go past it. The cops are gone. The house is quiet.

But I see her on the front porch. I see the way her head turns as I drive by.

And I see the way she lifts her hand to point at me.

26

AMANDA

My voice comes out as a croak as I watch the little red car zip through my neighborhood, driving faster than it should, hurrying away from me. "That's a red car."

But it's not the one from the hospital. It's not the one with the dented back bumper, which means it's not the boy I thought was following me. I lean against the house, drawing strength from how sturdy it is. "A red car," I murmur. "In my neighborhood."

It isn't a crime, but it feels like it should be.

The police are gone. After they pointed a gun at me as I tried to flee my own home, they apologized. They cleared the house. Nobody was in there.

One of the officers hosed off the muddy footprints on my porch while I gave my statement to another. He took copious notes but didn't seem too concerned.

He wasn't the one hiding in his bathroom, afraid that someone was in his house. Of course he wasn't too concerned. Anger rises in me, but I push it back down. It's one thing to be scared when you're out and about. There isn't a single woman in this world who hasn't been nervous when walking alone, especially at night. We've all had men approach us, tail us, all been afraid of what they might do.

But that's outside, and this was inside. I was terrified in my bathroom, fully convinced that someone was on the other side of the door, listening to me breathe, waiting for me to do something stupid that would allow them to get to me.

And even though the police have gone through every square foot of my house and have assured me that nothing is wrong, I can't shake the feeling that someone was in here with me. But it's not like when someone was in my office and I smelled jasmine. Nothing's moved. Things on my desk haven't been pushed around.

It's creepy.

Rubbing my arms to warm myself up, I decide to sit on the front porch in the sun. There's nothing like some natural heat to help me feel better than I do right now. After making some hot tea, I take it outside, then sit in my favorite rocking chair.

The neighborhood is busy. Down the street I hear some kids playing, and directly across from me, my neighbor is mowing his lawn. The sound is obnoxious, and I would normally go inside to escape it, but right now I want to be around other people, so I tuck my legs under me and take a sip of my tea.

Weed eaters, hedge trimmers, lawn mowers, kids laughing...all the normal sounds you'd expect from a neighborhood on a gorgeous Saturday morning. I can't shake the feeling that everyone is enjoying themselves, and I'm watching from the sidelines.

As I sit and stare off into space, a straw hat comes into view. Mr. Loren, the local curmudgeon and watchdog, makes his way down the street. He likes to make sure everyone's lawns are up to par and heads up the homeowners' association. Last summer my neighbor across the street got a notice in the mail from the association that her flowers were looking leggy and that she needed to trim them back.

It turned into an entire ordeal with her claiming that the plants were going to seed, which was good for local birds, but in the end a lawn care company came, mowed the lot down, and she was sent the bill.

Her house went on the market the next week.

Mr. Loren was behind it all, and as I watch him look around at the yards, I glance at mine, nervous. How does it look? Will he be able to find fault with it? Literally the last thing I can deal with right now is a notice in my mailbox that I'm going to be fined for something ridiculous, like low-hanging branches or a loose stone in my walkway.

I sink down in my chair.

"Amanda!" He stops in the road and waves.

Embarrassed, I sit up and wave back. Maybe he'll keep going. Maybe he won't want to talk about why the police were here. I stand up, wondering if I can make it into the house before he reaches me or speaks again.

"I need to talk to you! Don't run off now, you hear?"

"Dammit." I whisper the word, then plaster a fake smile on my face. "Mr. Loren, what can I do for you?" Hurrying, so I can meet him in the yard and not let him get close to a seat where he might be inclined to move in for the next hour or so, I rush down the steps and across the grass.

My feet sink into the wet grass and mud. It reminds me of the footprints on my porch this morning, and I push the thought away.

I'm fully expecting him to launch right into a litany of questions about what the police were doing at my house this morning and why I would disturb the peace with their lights and sirens, but what he says surprises me.

"There was someone strange in the neighborhood this

morning." He's walking with a cane, and he leans on it now, staring at me from under the brim of his hat.

I have a feeling he's waiting for me to confess that I was the strange person or that they were coming to my house.

But I have nothing to confess.

Nothing that I care to tell him, anyway.

"What happened?" My mouth is dry, and I take a sip of my tea.

"Some woman in a red car. Said she was lost and didn't have her GPS on, but I didn't like the cut of her. Shifty."

"What did she look like?" I speak as calmly as possible in an effort to sound calm, but the sharp glance he gives me tells me I failed.

"Shifty. Like I said. Why did you have the police here? A quiet neighborhood like this, there's really no reason to have them come by unless something bad is going on."

Should I tell him? If I come clean with Mr. Loren about why there were police at my house, then everyone on the street will know before I get back inside. He's got a knack for spreading information the way some people spread the flu.

"I thought I had an intruder," I tell him. "So I called them to come check it out."

He leans forward, his cane swaying with him. "You think she was in your house."

"No." The word flies from my lips before I have a chance to decide what I really think, but there's no taking it back now. "I think it's a coincidence."

"Hmm." He's watching me, his face serious. "Well, people do love to come look at the houses in this neighborhood. We run a pretty tight ship of making sure everyone's looks as nice as possible."

"That we do." I pause, considering. "But I thought you said she was lost."

"She wasn't lost. She was a looky-loo. They love to come

into high-quality neighborhoods and dream about the houses they can't afford. Maybe it has something to do with the letter." With that, he's done. Without even saying good-bye, he spins on his heel, slamming the tip of his cane down in front of him to help keep his balance. For a moment I think he's going down, but he rights himself, walking away from me without another word.

"What letter?" I call after him, but he still doesn't turn to respond. For a moment I watch him, racking my brain to come up with what in the world he was talking about. But I have no clue.

"Weird old man," I mutter, then turn back to my house. My tea is too cool for me now, and I dump it in the bushes before going inside.

I don't even manage to shut the front door before my phone starts to ring.

27

AMANDA

My hands shake as I spread the newspaper flat on the kitchen table and begin to slowly turn the pages, looking for the letters to the editor. The phone call I just received? Dr. Harris.

You definitely don't want a radiologist to call you on a Saturday morning after you've already had a visit from the police because you were afraid there was someone breaking into your house, but Dr. Harris wasn't calling about work. She was calling about a letter in the newspaper.

A letter about me.

Of course, I don't have the paper delivered to the house, but when I went online and looked for the letter she was talking about, I couldn't find it. Driving downtown and buying a paper out of the box made me feel like I was committing a crime even though I wasn't doing anything wrong.

Would someone recognize me? Would they know that I only wanted the paper because there was — apparently — something written about me in it?

"Please don't be from Belle Smith complaining about me

as a doctor," I mutter, licking my fingers and carefully turning another page. I hate the feeling of newspaper ink on my skin, but I ignore it as I scan the pages.

There.

I can honestly say that I don't think I've ever read a letter to the editor. It seems like a way for people to complain when they have no control over anything in their lives. Why someone would sit down and pen a complaint when they could get off their butts and do something about it is beyond me, but it seems that there's never any shortage of people wanting to hear themselves talk.

And there it is.

"Ooh, boy," I say, suddenly feeling chilled. I rub my hands together and roll my head back, cracking my neck as I take a few deep breaths. "Okay, Amanda, you've got this."

At first, I don't see the problem. I scan the letter quickly, not really reading what it says, more looking for any mention of my name. I must be scanning it too quickly. If I'm going to get to the bottom of why Dr. Harris would call me and tell me to go buy a paper, then I need to take my time and read every single word, no matter how painful that might be.

So I read it again. More slowly. This time I don't skim or skip over any words. I make sure I give every single one its due so I don't miss whatever the letter is trying to say.

"Dear Editor," I read, picking up the paper and folding it so I can more easily see the words. "I'm writing to expose an issue I faced at Mercy Heart during my first oncology appointment. Getting a cancer diagnosis is terrifying, as anyone who has had to go down that path can attest. The only thing that makes it bearable is knowing that you're going to have a great team working with you and for you to protect you."

Okay, right now I don't see the problem. Someone got a cancer diagnosis, which is terrible. But Dr. Harris didn't tell me that the letter was a glowing review of my treatment. My stomach turns when I picture Belle Smith.

I keep reading, my voice quiet in the still of my kitchen.

"Of course, I wanted treatment from the best of the best, and that is why I searched out Dr. Morgan." *There it is.* "Unfortunately for me, as well as for any other patient she might have had that day, Dr. Morgan was not performing at her best. She did not have my chart that I needed from my doctor, she was unable to give me a personalized treatment plan, and she told me that I'd have to come back in to obtain that information."

I'm starting to see red. Closing my eyes, I force a few deep breaths into my lungs. "Everything I did at that appointment was to make her feel better." My teeth are gritted. I don't want to read the rest of the letter, but it can't be any worse.

It is.

"Mercy Heart has an incredible reputation for taking care of its patients and making sure that we receive the best possible care, but Dr. Morgan and her entire staff dropped the ball. A patient shouldn't be blamed for not having their chart when they go to the doctor. They shouldn't be required to come back at another time for an additional appointment. In no way should patients be treated the way I was when I was at my most vulnerable."

I suck in a breath.

"I don't know what my future holds. I've reached out to Mercy Heart and filed an official complaint with the board but haven't heard back about what kind of action they are going to take against Dr. Morgan to ensure that no patient is ever treated the way I was. I know we can't go back in time to undo how I was treated, just like we can't go back in time to undo my diagnosis. I will move forward and find someone to treat me and give me the care I need. I only hope to prevent other people from dealing with the same frustrating experience that I had to endure with Dr. Morgan."

A forceful exhale. I feel like my lungs have fully deflated. My hands are sweaty, and I force myself to put the paper back down on the table. There's more. I don't want to read it.

But I have to.

"I'm begging anyone who needs cancer treatment to reconsider their options. I'm begging the hospital board to more closely examine what happened at my appointment. And I'm begging Dr. Morgan, who may be a brilliant oncologist in her own right but absolutely doesn't have the right to treat patients the way she treated me, to reconsider her bedside manner. I hope this letter will help current and future patients not only access the care they need, but also the care they deserve."

It's signed *Belle Smith*.

"This bitch." I sit back in my chair, the tension that I was holding in my body suddenly gone. I wipe my hand across my forehead; it's slick with sweat. Around me the air feels thick. Sticky. I want to move, to be outside where I can at least breathe some clean air into my lungs, but I don't dare do it.

I highly doubt other neighbors don't read the paper. Mr. Loren already mentioned it, a casual barb thrown over his shoulder. When I think about how many of them might have already read this letter about me, especially if he pointed them in its direction, I want to throw up.

"Okay, Amanda, okay." Planting my hands on the table, I force myself to stand. I'm unbalanced and keep one hand on the table for support. "Okay. This Belle wants to ruin your career. Why? Who the hell is she?"

I have to figure this out. It's only a matter of time before someone at the hospital calls me, wanting to know what the hell happened. To receive a complaint from her, that was bad enough. But to have her reach out to the paper like this, to have her throw me under the bus publicly?

It's enough to make me feel like I need to pull out my hair.

"Think about the people you've wronged." I say the words to try to force myself to do it, no matter how hard it's going to be. It's one thing to know you've hurt or upset people in the past, another to face that head-on. I don't want to think about whom I might have hurt, but what choice do I have?

I have to get to the bottom of this.

Of course I've lost patients in the past. That's the way these things go when your job is to fight cancer. There will always be a time when the cancer is found too late. When it's metastasized. When it's spread so quickly, so quietly and insidiously, that the only way to remove it all would be to kill the patient.

Those times happen, but that's not what this is. It doesn't *feel* right. Families understand when we lose a patient that we all feel the same pain they do. They know how hard I fight, the long hours I put in. They see me crying behind my mask.

So this isn't that. This isn't some family member who lost a loved one and now wants revenge. Besides, I haven't lost a patient in...well, a few years. It's a good track record in my line of work.

There's only one way to resolve this, and that's to find Belle before she can strike at me again. I have to learn what it is about me that she hates so much, why she wants to hurt me. I have to figure this out, and then I have to stop her.

I grab my keys and wallet.

Her address is stuck in my mind. I know it's fake. It has to be fake. But sitting around the house waiting for her to strike again isn't going to do me any good.

It's time to go on the offensive.

28

COLLETTE

It's been an hour since I drove into Amanda's neighborhood, saw the police clustered outside her house, saw the way she lifted her hand and pointed right at me. I shiver when I think about the expression on her face.

Did she *see* me? Is it possible that she put two and two together and really knows who I am? I don't know how well she could see my face, or if she had any idea that we've met before in her office. There was no way to tell how the shadows fell on my windows, if they did enough to block my face, or if she was pointing.

Maybe she *thought* she knew who I was. I highly doubt she was able to see my face, but still...the thought makes me tremble in fear again.

"I wish you could have seen it, Henry," I say, picking him up and slinging him over my shoulder like a purse. He used to scream at me when I did that, but that was when Arabella was still alive. Now he takes my loving abuse. We both know that we're the only two who will put up with each other.

"She looked devastated. And the police were at her

house." He meows in my ear, and I snuggle him closer, kissing him on the top of his head before dumping him on the sofa. "Do you think she called about my muddy footprints?"

That had been a stroke of genius. I'd wanted to see inside her house, but she keeps the blinds shut, making it really difficult to see much of anything. Last night one of the blind slats had gotten snagged, and I could see a sliver of her living room. It was boring.

I'd love to watch her in her space, her bedroom, her kitchen. I'd love to see her when her defenses are down. Does she think about Arabella? Does she think about killing her? Does she regret it?

Probably not, judging by the wine I saw her drinking at Tito's and the amount of glass recycling she sent out this past week.

My feet hadn't been muddy when I went up onto the porch to look in her windows, but then I saw how wet the lawn was, how there was a patch of mud right there by the porch, and I stepped in it. It was like I was a kid again, playing in the mud, purposefully making my shoes filthy.

I didn't want her to catch me on her porch, but I wanted her to know I'd been there when she got up. I needed her to not only see my footprints, but to worry about what they meant.

And I'd wager that's exactly what happened if she was willing to call the police. Someone like her, someone who faked their own death, must have been pretty terrified to reach out to the police.

I love it.

She seemed so unflappable when I was in her office for my appointment. The thought that I could work my way under her skin enough for her to call the police in fear? Well, that's delicious. It puts to shame any plans I have for the rest of the day.

It's gorgeous out, though, so while I don't mind the thought of sitting inside with Henry and hanging out with a good book, I think I'm going to head downtown. I have things to celebrate. Not only did I upset Amanda enough to make her ring the police, but my letter to the editor was in the paper, so surely someone important will have seen it by now.

I think I'll buy two more copies. One for me, one for her. After the sun sets tonight, I'll swing by her house and drop it in her mailbox. There's no way I want to risk her not reading the wonderful letter I wrote about her, and this will ensure she does. It's a risk, sure, but aren't all good things in life?

I'm not going to sit back and hope things go my way. No, that never works out the way you want it to. I'm going to grab life by the horns and force it into the shape I want.

That thought in mind, I send Jackson a text. A coffee downtown sounds amazing to me, and if I have the opportunity to meet with a friend and celebrate my latest success, then all the better.

Fifteen minutes later I'm sitting at Java Chip, an oversized cup of black coffee for me, a latte waiting for him. Jackson seemed thrilled when he responded to my text and told me he'd meet me here as soon as he could put on some shoes. Each time the door opens, I look up in anticipation, but so far it's been a group of wannabe teenage goths, two frazzled yoga moms, and a man who's definitely having an affair.

I watched as he slipped his wedding band from his finger and put it in his pocket before meeting a woman who looks half his age. Smirking, I turn back to my coffee. People are all the same, no matter how old they are or where they're from. We all want security, to be loved, and to be surrounded by things that make us happy.

When that's not happening, then that's when we start to look outside ourselves for validation. This man slipping off his wedding band probably has a lovely family waiting for him at home. They probably don't have any idea he's a cheater and that he's so willing to throw away his vows, but here he is.

I'm mildly curious about whether or not the girl he's meeting knows that he's married, but before I can eavesdrop on their conversation, Jackson walks through the door. He looks around the coffee shop, then smiles when he sees me. I grin back like a fool as he threads his way through the chairs.

"Got you a latte," I tell him, gesturing to the drink. "And something else."

"Oh?" He sits down next to me and takes a sip of his drink. Sighing with pleasure, he puts it down and then turns his full attention to me. "What in the world do you have that you think could be better than this latte?"

"This." Flipping the paper around so he can read the letter, I tap it to make him look. "It's printed, Jackson." I lower my voice even though I'm pretty sure nobody is paying attention to me. "It looks so good, don't you think?"

He doesn't answer right away, and I sit back, watching him read. His eyes flick back and forth quickly as he tears through what I've written. I don't even realize that I'm holding my breath until he smiles, puts the paper down, and looks up at me.

"This is good."

"You think?"

He nods, and I relax even more. My coffee is cool enough for me to drink it without burning my tongue, and I take a long sip, closing my eyes as I imagine the caffeine hitting my bloodstream.

"I thought you were going to write about her changing her identity." He sounds confused. When he slides the newspaper across the table to me, I take it and fold it back up before I answer.

"I thought about it. I thought this would be better. It would hopefully end with having her investigated, getting the news to look into her as a doctor, then maybe seeing that she's been lying about who she really is." I pause. Did I make a mistake? Did I totally blow it?

That thought makes my heart beat faster. I don't want to contemplate even for a moment that I might have stabbed myself in the foot and ruined my chance to see Amanda thrown in jail where she belongs.

But maybe I did.

"Oh, God." I drop my head into my hands. "Oh, God, Jackson, I messed up, didn't I? This was my one chance to call attention to her and what she's been up to and who she really is, and I...threw it away."

"You can write another one," he says, but I shake my head.

"No, I can't. You know it. If I keep writing to them about the same person, then I doubt anyone's going to take me seriously." I'm spiraling. The quiet hum and chatter in the coffee shop was comforting, but now it's making me feel like I can't think straight. I stand up, leaving my coffee on the table.

"Where are you going?" Jackson stands too, mirroring me, only he picks up his latte like he's unwilling to leave it behind. "Are you okay? You look pale, Collette. Let's talk it out."

"There's nothing to talk about." Even to my ears, my voice sounds tight. Strained. "I messed up, Jackson. I had one chance, and I blew it. I wrote the complaint to the hospital, then thought I should follow up with a letter to the editor, and now what am I going to do? I have to make people see what she's done and who she really is, and I don't know how to do that."

My voice has gotten louder as it's gotten higher, and I suddenly stop, turning around to see how many people are looking at me.

Quite a few of them. Not the man with the wedding ring, but I sense very few things could pull his attention away from the girl sitting across from him.

"Hey, Collette, let's take a breath, okay? You're okay." Jackson is calm. Too calm.

I can't handle being around someone calm right now.

"I have to go." My keys are already in my hand. When did I pluck them from my purse? Before he can think about stopping me, I'm hurrying away from the table, pushing my way past assorted customers, finally bursting through the front door into the fresh air.

I have no idea what I'm going to do, but I have to salvage this. Amanda killed my sister, and now she has the perfect life.

She has gotten away with murder for too long.

There's only one thing left that I can do to her.

I'll make her confess what she did. I'll make her turn herself in; then finally she'll be in prison, where she belongs.

29

AMANDA

I pull up in front of the butcher's and kill my engine, sitting in silence as I stare at the windows. They're almost floor to ceiling, perfect for displaying enormous cuts of meat. Some skinless animal hangs right up front, the fat so white that it's almost too white, the flesh bright red.

My stomach turns.

I've never been to this butcher because I prefer to buy my meat, when I do eat it, in Styrofoam trays. I don't want to see it still on the bone, and certainly don't want to listen to the thunk of a cleaver as it's cut for me.

But this is the address Belle Smith put on her patient information sheet, so I'm here. It's obvious she lied, I knew that before I got in the car, but I still have questions.

I'm out of place in the shop, and I have to wait for a line of customers to clear. Right when I'm about to walk up to the counter and ask a man in a stained apron some questions, a man with a toddler comes in, and I step to the side. I can wait. I have all day.

Finally, it's my turn, and I take a deep breath before

speaking. It smells in here, coppery, like blood, but also like death. My nose burns.

"Flank steak is on sale," the man says before I can utter a word.

"I'm sorry?"

"Flank steak." Turning, he pulls a piece of steak from the cooler behind him and holds it up in the air for me to see. "You look like a flank steak girl."

"I'm more of a tofu girl," I tell him. "But I was hoping I could ask you some questions."

The meat makes a sick sound as he drops it back where it was. "About?" He crosses his dense, freckled arms.

I can't help but notice the specks of blood on them, and I force myself to look up at his face.

"Are there apartments around here?"

A blank stare.

I'm going to have to give him more if he's to meet me halfway. "Someone gave me her address, and I think she made a mistake. This is the one she gave me, but it's pretty clear there aren't apartments here."

"Pretty clear," he agrees. "You sure she wasn't giving you a fake address to keep you at bay? Like sometimes women will give fake phone numbers?"

Oh, he thinks I'm looking for a woman I want to date. "It's not like that. We're not dating, we're friends."

Nothing.

"I was supposed to drop some stuff off at her house, but she's not picking up her phone, and she clearly doesn't live here unless you have her in the walk-in freezer in the back."

I smile to lighten the mood. He doesn't.

"I'm sorry," he finally says, obviously deciding I'm not really a threat to whoever I'm trying to find. "This place wasn't ever an apartment, and the only ones anywhere near here are across the river. Not sure where she was trying to tell you to go, but I guarantee you it wasn't here."

"Okay. Great." It's not great, but I can't argue with this man. "I really appreciate your help. Good luck with the flank steak sale." Before he can ask me one more time if I want to buy anything, I hurry back outside and into my rental. I don't want meat. I don't want to be here for another second if I can help it. What I want is my car back. I want to know who Belle Smith really is; she didn't show up online in the searches I did for her.

But mostly I want to know what she wants from me. It's too much of a coincidence — all of this. Even though I knew in my gut that I shouldn't have let her come into my office to be seen as a patient without her chart, I did it anyway, because that's the kind of doctor I am.

And now look at where that's gotten me. A formal complaint filed against me at the hospital. Thank goodness they're not taking it seriously, not beyond trying to contact her, which I'm assuming has failed miserably. Then there's the letter to the editor. That's far more damning; that's something out there in the community.

Everyone knows that when you want to bring someone to their knees, you do it in public. It's a public shaming, as close as she can come to putting my face up on a huge billboard and broadcasting my make-believe sins to the entire town.

A chill runs through me when I think about that. She's crazy. I didn't pick up on it when I first met her because I was so worried about taking care of a patient, but this woman is completely off her rocker, and for some reason, she has me in her sights.

"What next?" I turn out of the butcher's and head back towards town, back to the area I'm more familiar with. There has to be something I can do, some way I can stop her, but I don't know what that will be if I can't even find the woman.

She's like a ghost, and the fact that she's around but impossible for me to pin down is enough to drive me over the edge.

I should hire a lawyer. Surely someone in this little town would be able to help me out, would be able to make her stop. There has to be someone who could file a cease and desist, or whatever it would take to make this harassment stop.

But there's only one problem with that. I know who's causing these problems. I've sat down and talked with her, taken her by the shoulders and looked deep into her eyes as I've promised her that I was going to take care of her.

But that woman doesn't exist. Belle Smith doesn't exist, which means I can't very well find her to stop her. I'm going to have to wait for her to show her face again; then I'm going to be able to bring this to a close.

That means I need to be vigilant.

I need to make sure she's not able to one-up me again. It's going to be exhausting, to be looking over my shoulder every time I go somewhere, but what other choice do I have? Either I keep an eye out for this woman and somehow stop her from ruining my life, or she's going to go ahead and do whatever she wants to me.

I tap mindlessly on the steering wheel as I drive. Cars zip around me. Everyone is in a hurry except me. I don't have anywhere to go, not really. I can go home. Hide there. Wait until I need to head back to the hospital for work.

The thought of locking myself in my house to stay away from this woman is depressing. I'm about to turn into my neighborhood when I see it.

A flash of red.

I straighten my wheel back out. Screw going home. I'm following that little red car.

30

COLLETTE

Driving always clears my head.

There's something about the rhythmic sound of my tires on the road, the way my car moves carefully through curves, something about how the radio sounds immersive when I turn it up.

It makes me feel like I'm not really here, like everything terrible that I've been handling has fallen away and I can finally relax. Amanda wasn't home when I swung by her house, but it's not like I really expected her to be. What, did I think she'd have all the lights or a big sign on the door proclaiming that she was around and waiting for me to arrive?

No, I didn't.

I'm still disappointed, though. After leaving the coffee shop and ignoring Jackson as he chased after me, I got in the car and drove. I didn't mean to end up in her neighborhood. I know I need to be careful about coming here too much, that the neighbors will start to become suspicious.

Thank goodness I didn't run into the man with the straw

hat again. As much as I'd like to think he didn't suspect anything when I was driving down the road, I know how some people are. I saw the way he looked at me, like he thinks everyone is guilty until proven innocent.

But I didn't see him. I didn't see anyone, actually, which was nice. It's probably for the better that Amanda wasn't home since I don't know what I'm going to do to her. All I know is she deserves to be punished. I thought all of my hard work so far would be enough to make other people see how evil she is, but apparently I'm wrong.

I'm going to have to work harder to punish her. She's not going to be found guilty in the court of public opinion, and as much as I thought I would have some help from the hospital or townspeople, I don't know if that is going to happen.

Jackson's right. I should have written about what she did to Arabella. At least then I could rely on some journalist looking for their big break to pick up the story. As it is, any journalist who reaches out to the hospital for a statement will be told that Belle Smith is a disgruntled patient, someone who has a grudge for some reason, someone whom they can't even get in contact with to see if my claims are true.

I messed up.

"Dammit." Pulling into the cemetery parking lot, I kill my engine and then lean forward, putting my head down on the steering wheel. I don't normally come visit Arabella on Saturday, but right now I need to talk to my sister. I know that I can't ever do that again, but that doesn't mean I can't come and spend time with her.

She's dead.

I know that.

I know that coming here isn't going to bring her back.

But it should at least stop the pounding in my head that's making it so difficult for me to think straight.

The air here is cooler, something I attribute to the thick woods surrounding the cemetery. There are two cemeteries in town, and this is the one I chose for Arabella. The other is on top of a hill, which means it has great views, but there's no shade in the summer. There's no cool breeze sweeping down through the woods, and that was something I knew Arabella would miss.

It's silly, isn't it? The lengths we go to to make sure our loved ones are comfortable even though they're gone? Logically I know that Arabella isn't here. I know she has no idea about how loamy the earth smells after a good rain. She will never again see the way the clouds can filter down among the trees, a thick fog that is difficult to see through.

But I still wanted her here. I wanted her to be somewhere I knew she would love if she were still alive. She deserved to rest under the beauty of trees, with ferns growing around the corner, not somewhere hot and baking and that she wouldn't have really wanted to visit when she was still alive. So I buried her here.

My feet walk the familiar path to her grave. I'd have loved it if I walked a small hiking path, wandering through the woods, to see her headstone, but the paths are wider than that. They have to be accessible; it has to be possible for everyone who lost someone to come here and see the person they loved.

I understand.

It's not what I wanted for my sister.

None of this was.

I find her grave, all alone, the plots next to her not yet sold. When I have some extra money, I want to buy one next to hers so I can rest with her after I die. Hopefully that won't be anytime soon, but you never know. It's not worth waiting to see what's going to happen, not when you can prepare.

There was a gentle rain the other day, and the ground is still a little muddy, so I spread my jacket on some moss next to her headstone before sitting down. The jacket is old and used to be waterproof, but it's not any longer. Not that I care about being a bit damp. Being in a cemetery puts things into perspective for you.

"Hey," I say, picking up a fallen stick and picking off some of the bark. It lodges under my nail and looks like dirt. "I wanted to come by. I miss you." My voice breaks.

The wind shifts and brings with it the sound of someone crying.

"I'm doing everything I can to make things right for you," I tell Arabella. "I know I can't ever bring you back, that's silly of me to even think it. I know you're dead and gone, and she's still alive, breathing, eating, enjoying her life. I've tried really hard to forgive her."

That's a lie. Never once have I thought about forgiveness. It's all been revenge.

"But I don't know that I can." I clear my throat. "Anyway, Henry hasn't thrown up in my shoes in a while, although he did fall jumping off the sofa the other day. It ended up with him hitting his head on the floor. I think he's okay, but I still called the vet. They said it might be a seizure? I don't know."

I have to keep Henry alive. He's all I have left of my sister. Coming here and talking to her bones isn't the same. It won't ever be the same.

"I'm doing my best, okay? Not solely for Henry, but for myself. But she doesn't deserve to be alive, and you do. I wanted to let you know what I'm going to do."

If Arabella were alive, she'd do her best to talk me out of everything I'm planning, but that's the rub, isn't it? She's not. So even though I know my sister wouldn't agree with my plan, even though I know she'd do whatever it took to stop me, I tell her what I'm thinking.

I go through my entire plan, growing more and more animated as I do. Thank goodness she had enough life insurance to buy this plot way up out of the main part of the cemetery.

I can only imagine what people would think if they were to hear me talking right now.

31

AMANDA

The red car pulls into the grocery store, and I turn in behind it. I'm trying to hang back some so I don't have to worry about them realizing that they're being followed; but if they know, they don't seem to care. The car parks towards the back of the lot. It's ridiculously busy here, and they're blocked in on all sides.

Except they'll still be able to back out.

Anger rushes through me, and I pull to a stop right behind their car. People are going to honk at me to move, I know that, but I throw my car into park, ready to hurry up to the driver's side of the red car before they can leave.

They can't go anywhere. I have them completely blocked in, and a flash of triumph shoots through me. I want to hurt this person. Whoever it is who's ruining my life, I want to make them stop. The public parking lot isn't the best place for a showdown, but I can't help that.

I saw them driving past my neighborhood. It has to be the person who's out to get me.

Only I'm going to get them first.

I slam my door and race around the front of my car, my

eyes locked on the red car. From here I can see the driver, see the way they're looking around like they're lost. *Or looking for a way out.*

I'm going to stop them. This isn't the best plan I've ever had, but I can't let someone continue to harass me.

Belle Smith, whoever she really is, is going to stop now.

Raising my fist, I prepare to bang on the window to make the person come out, but the door opens as I walk up to it. A small foot clad in a sensible brown shoe lightly touches the ground, and I stop as a woman steps out.

She has a perfect white perm, her hair like a halo around her head. One hand clutches her purse, a sensible brown thing that matches her shoes; the other holds onto the door of the car like she needs the support. For a moment she doesn't say anything, just takes me in, her eyes flicking up and down my body like she's scanning me for something.

Then she smiles.

"Dr. Morgan?" There's a tremble to her voice that makes it difficult for me to understand her at first, then I realize what she said, and my heart drops.

"Mrs. Garret?" I didn't recognize her at first, didn't recognize my patient from years ago, but now I do. She's aged, but haven't we all. She's still upright and above ground, the one thing she asked me to do for her when she came to me for treatment for her breast cancer.

"Oh, I can't believe I'm so lucky to run into you here!" Before I know what she's doing, she flings her arms around me, pulling me close.

I pause for a moment, trying to collect my thoughts, then hug her back.

"You know, I begged you to help me stay alive for the birth of my first grandchild, and now I have four."

"Oh, Mrs. Garret," I say, carefully extracting myself from her grasp, "that's amazing. That's incredible, truly."

I'd pulled into this parking lot behind the red car wanting nothing more than to ram it. I wanted to hit the car so hard from the back that it would spin around, slam into a wall, burst into flames. My rage was strong enough to turn my stomach, and even now I clench my fists to try to tamp down the feeling.

"Thank you, dear." Reaching up, she lightly cups my cheek and gives a quiet chuckle. "Thank you for giving me my life back. How wonderful to run into you here."

"It is." I gesture back at my car. Frustrated drivers keep having to take turns going around it, and I give a sympathetic wave. "I saw you and had to pull in to talk to you."

"Aren't you a dear? I would love to stay and chat, but I promised my daughter Elise that I'd swing in, pick up some baby food for the youngest, and then be right home. He's a chunky little thing; you'd love to squeeze his cheeks. I'm so glad you stopped to say hello, Doctor. Really, it was good to see you. Take care." She takes my hands in hers and gives them a hard squeeze before turning and winding her way through the parked cars to the store.

All I can do is stand and stare after her. I was so convinced whoever was in that car was the person driving me insane, but now I take a deep breath and look around the parking lot.

Red cars are scattered everywhere like confetti. I feel my heart sink.

What if I'd let the thoughts in my head get the best of me? What if I'd actually hit Mrs. Garret's car and spun it off the road like I'd wanted to? What if I'd done that and murdered her?

Someone is following me. Someone, this Belle Smith, wants to drive me insane, but she wasn't the one in the red car just now.

"Oh, God." The full gravity of what happened and how

willing I was to hurt an innocent person hits me, and I turn around, leaning against Mrs. Garret's car. I rub my hands up and down my arms. The day is warming up, the sun bright overhead, but I have to get a grip.

I have to stop this.

Belle Smith is trying to hurt me, but I can't stoop to her level. What if I accidentally hurt someone like old Mrs. Garret? How in the world would I live with myself then?

A doctor's oath is to do no harm. That's something I've always lived by when practicing medicine. Of course, there are accidents. Of course, there are some things I wish I could take back, some patients I wish I could have saved even though there really wasn't any way for me to do that by the time they came to me.

We all have regrets.

I'm not going to add to mine.

32

COLLETTE

Group this week feels subdued. Or maybe it's me. I feel like I'm walking through water, like every interaction I have is quieter than it's supposed to be. It's like a dense fog has descended on the world, and I'm the only one who's affected. Nobody else seems to be bothered by it; nobody else seems to feel like they're right on the verge of drowning.

Henry had a full-blown seizure last night. I ended up rushing him to the emergency vet, but by the time I got him there, it was over, and he was fine. Well, that's what they said.

They sent me home with a gabapentin prescription and told me to keep an eye on him. He's woozy, not quite himself. When Arabella was still alive, I would have loved for him to be taken down a notch, for him to be less of a pain to me when I came around, but now I don't want that.

I want him living his life to the fullest, even if that means being a bit of a terror in the house. The vet told me I could cut back on the gabapentin to make him feel more like himself, but to remember that it was the only thing keeping him from having a seizure.

My throat feels like it's going to close up. I must make some sort of noise because I feel a hand on mine, fingers lacing into mine, and I look over into Linda's smiling face.

"Today is really hard for you, isn't it? Is it an anniversary?"

An anniversary of Arabella's death, she means. Everyone likes to talk in code when dealing with trauma and sorrow.

I shake my head. There's no good way to tell anyone here that the reason I'm not feeling my best is because of a stupid cat that I used to hate but who is now all I have left of my sister.

Who would understand that? Nobody, that's who.

"Collette, do you have anything to share? Mark here is new, and I know he'd love some tips on how to make it through your days without allowing grief to overtake you." Vince stares at me, gesturing to the man next to him.

Mark is young. Too young to be at grief group, but that's probably what people say about me. He has an aura of loss around him, and the expression on his face is so uncomfortable that I don't even want to make eye contact with him.

"I think the most important thing to remember is that your loved ones would want you to be happy." I hear the words coming out of my mouth even though I don't realize I'm saying them. It's something I read in a grief book that Carol handed me when I first started counseling.

I can spout off the wisdom with the best of them, but that doesn't mean I believe any of it.

"And when you feel like you're drowning, you have to draw strength from somewhere. Maybe that's art or cooking or music. You need to find some sort of passion that will allow you to have a focus during your hardest days."

It's all a load of crap. The only thing that helps me focus when I'm missing Arabella so badly is hating the woman who killed her. My focus is Amanda Morgan, much-loved physician, and much-hated murderer.

Gavin smiles.

When you do enough reading of the materials handed to you, then it's easy to regurgitate whatever it is people want to hear. What I actually want to say to this new guy would probably end up with me kicked out of group.

It would probably result in me going back to one-on-one therapy with Carol.

I want to tell him that the pain he's feeling right now will never go away. It will never decrease. He'll never wake up one morning suddenly feeling less alone than he was before he went to bed. The grief doesn't shrink. It doesn't become easier to live with.

You learn to suffer with it. It's like a splinter wedged so far into you that not even the most skilled surgeon would ever be able to remove it. Instead of growing out of the grief or your body wearing it down, you grow around it. You develop callouses, scar tissue. Your body holds onto it, and it becomes part of you.

The grief doesn't change in size or in depth. It never stops making you feel like you're going to drown, and it never lessens in intensity. You learn to deal with it. You learn how to move through life with this splinter lodged in your heart.

Until you move and it shifts, and it all comes crashing back down around you again, all of it so painful that it's like the very first day when you lost the person you love. And then you're forced to start back over, building up the scar tissue, trying to form callouses.

And then, one day, if you're not careful, the grief will kill you. I haven't been a member of grief group very long, but I've heard the whispers about Willa, how she couldn't handle losing her baby, and she killed herself. The grief will either force you to take your own life when you're still young, or you'll die with it lodged in you like a stake.

I know I'm going to die from my grief, but I'm going to take Amanda out with me.

After group, while I'm eating a donut and staring out the window, Jackson approaches me. It's the first time we've spoken since I left him at the coffee shop over the weekend. He reached out a few times, sending texts that went unanswered, but now he's here again, and I turn my body to let him know I see him.

"How are you?" His voice is quiet, not only because he wants to make sure nobody else hears our conversation, but because I'm skittish. I saw myself in the mirror this morning, saw how wide my eyes are. I know how I look to the people in group.

"Fine. Disappointed." I hesitate, taking another bite to buy some time while I think. "I feel like I lost my chance to ruin her life when I wrote the letter to the editor."

"Do you feel better now?"

"About what? Writing the wrong thing or trying to heal through the letter?"

He doesn't answer.

"No, I don't feel better." I want to tell him about Henry, but how I feel about Henry isn't something I can explain to anyone. "I messed up, Jackson. I had this amazing opportunity to show the world what she's really like, and I blew it, and now if I try again with another letter, it would come across like I'm some crazy woman."

"I know."

"But I'm not crazy."

"I also know that. Listen, Collette, maybe we're going about this the wrong way. Maybe you need to talk to someone about this. Maybe there's a better way to handle what you're feeling."

I stare at him, unable to believe what he's saying. He's been so supportive this entire time, always looking out for me and letting me know that I'm not alone in how I feel. Jackson was the first person — no, the only person — who didn't think I was crazy for believing that Courtney Barrow is still walking around alive. And now he wants me to give it all up?

"I don't think I can do that," I say. Each word is measured, weighed, and carefully spoken. It's imperative to me that he understand how I feel right now. "Jackson, I'm too far gone down this path. I need you to understand it. If you could bring your wife back, would you do it? Would you hurt anyone who ever made her suffer before she died?"

There's a flash of something on his face, but the expression is too fleeting for me to grasp what it is. I want to go back, rewind the moment, do my best to parse out what he was thinking, but there's no way to do that.

"If you think she's really her, Collette, if Amanda is Courtney and she's the reason Arabella is dead, then you have to do what is right for you. And for your sister."

He's not agreeing with me, not fully, but I don't need him to give me permission for what I need to do. I knew it when I left the coffee shop this weekend. I knew it when I was talking to Arabella at the cemetery.

And I know it now. Jackson doesn't want to help me with what I'm doing, but I wouldn't ask him to anyway.

Revenge for Arabella won't remove the splinter in my heart, but it will make it a lot more bearable, and right now I'm willing to do anything to ease this pain.

33

AMANDA

I'm not sure that a lot of people would ever be able to understand how much peace I enjoy from sitting by my daughter's grave. I'm sure there are a number of people in the world who, once they bury someone they love, never return. Maybe going to the graveside is too difficult for them. Maybe they think that they can't ever be close to the person they lost.

But I know they're wrong. I've seen enough death in my professional life to know how to handle it, and that's why I visit my daughter every single week. The calla lilies I put in her gravestone's vase look stunning, bright and cheery. Part of me feels bad for the other graves here without flowers, without anyone to visit them.

I pull a blue rock from my pocket and put it on the ground by her headstone. One of my patients left it with me, saying that it brought her good luck. She's in remission now, so I guess it worked.

What did she call it? Azurite. It means nothing to me, but it's the type of thing I could have imagined my daughter filling her pocket with and bringing home to me if she were ever lucky enough to stumble on a cache of rocks like this.

Or lucky enough to grow that old.

It doesn't matter how much time has passed since she died; I'll always remember what it was like to hold her when she was first born, and will always hate the fact that I'm not able to do that any longer.

It happens. That was what the medical examiner told me. The police parroted it to me, but only after a thorough examination to make sure I hadn't hurt her. I didn't. I *couldn't.* There wasn't anything in this world that brought me as much joy and happiness as she did, and I wouldn't have ever snuffed out her life on purpose.

"You would have loved this movie I saw on television last night," I tell her, running my fingers over the moss that has slowly grown over her grave. There are other plots in this cemetery that are in the shade, and the moss would have grown faster over her grave, but I wanted her to have some sun on her during parts of the day. "It was about a cat and two dogs that get lost and then have to work together to find their way back home."

What I don't say and wouldn't admit to anyone is that I cried my eyes out watching it. I can't even tell Greta how much the movie upset me, how much it made me want her.

"Anyway, things are kinda crazy with work, but you don't have to worry, I'll be back next week. Maybe I'll bring another rock. That could be our thing."

I could choose bright ones that looked like a rainbow on the ground. She'd have liked that, and I love the idea of my sweet girl covered up with a rainbow for the rest of time.

Sighing, I stand up and leave, brushing my hands on my pants. It's a short walk back to the parking lot.

I'm almost to my car when I freeze.

There's a red car here, parked three spaces down from

where I parked. My first response is to run for my car, throw the door open, then lock it after me. I want to race out of here, make sure that whoever followed me here isn't going to hurt me.

"But that's me being paranoid," I tell myself, giving my head a shake. "A red car here doesn't mean anything, and it certainly doesn't mean that someone is following you." I'm doing this thing where I talk myself down off the ledge. Red cars have been freaking me out, but for no real good reason.

Nothing terrible has happened yet. People drive red cars, and that doesn't mean I should panic each time I see one.

Still, my heart hammers in my chest.

I take a deep breath and walk past my car. Past the next car. And the next. I stop at the red car, eyeballing it.

The red car doesn't have any damage on its back bumper.

I have no way of knowing if I've ever seen it before, but I bet I haven't.

The fact that they have an in-state plate doesn't even mean that they're from here. It's entirely possible that whoever drove the red car came through for the same reason I did, to see someone they loved.

"I have to stop thinking like this," I mutter to myself, turning in a slow circle. There's one other car here, but, as I watch, an older couple holding hands appears from another part of the cemetery. They get in their car and drive away. If someone were following me, wouldn't they be watching me right now? Wouldn't they be hiding behind the car or a tree so they could leap out at me?

I turn quickly, jumping completely around, trying to catch whoever is watching me.

Nobody's there.

"I'm losing my mind." It feels terrible to say, worse to believe, but nobody followed me to the cemetery. Nobody's been watching me, tailing me, coming by my house...

Except for the footprints.

Except for Mr. Loren telling me about the person in a red car on the street.

The temperature seems to plummet ten degrees, and I shiver, wrapping my arms around my body as I hurry to my car.

Sometimes, even when you don't want to believe it, the worst is true. I don't want to believe that there's a person in a red car following me around town, stalking me, looking in the windows of my home. I don't want to think that a woman who isn't really even my patient has it in for me for some reason.

But what else am I to believe?

When all evidence points to one truth, then you should probably believe it, even if the truth seems to be so far-fetched that it's almost laughable. Even when I try and try to convince myself that nothing sinister is going on.

The problem is, no matter how much I don't want to think it's true, whoever is out to harass me seems to know a lot about me. And I know nothing about them.

34

COLLETTE

I'm holding my breath as Amanda walks to her car. She'd spun in a slow circle, obviously on the lookout for anyone who might be watching her, then jumped around like she was going to be able to move fast enough to catch me.

But I'm in the shadows. They hide me, and I stare at her, my mouth dropping open slightly as she hurries to her car, reverses, then flies out of the parking lot. It's the second time I've seen her come here, and now that I know for sure she's gone, I hurry in the direction she came from.

Calla lilies. They're gorgeous, and I reach out, lightly running my finger along the edge of one of them. Kneeling, I reach out and touch the name carved in the headstone.

Greta Morgan

The dates are so close together that my breath catches in my throat. "You were a little thing," I say, reaching down and picking up a small blue rock by her gravestone. "Such a tiny little thing and now you're gone."

From somewhere in the woods ahead of me, a bird calls. I sit very still, soaking up the sun and thinking hard about what I need to do next. Of course, I feel for Amanda that she lost this little girl, whoever she was. Greta was young, but I have no idea who she was while she was still alive. Family? Did she have a daughter, a niece? That's the only real explanation for why she'd come here on a regular basis to see her.

It explains why she'd come to the cemetery, but knowing that she's felt loss like this doesn't make me feel bad for her. She should have understood how killing my sister would make me feel. She should have killed herself, really done it, not pretended and lied about it.

"You bring death with you wherever you go, don't you?"

I stand, slipping the rock into my pocket. It's not heavy, but I feel it there like a weight pulling me down to the ground.

The flowers on the grave are next. I'm not going to take them home to enjoy them, just take them so Amanda knows I was here. Nobody deserves flowers from that woman. I'll dump them in a trash can on my way through town, and nobody will be the wiser.

Maybe someone else would learn that Amanda had lost a daughter and change how they felt about her. Maybe someone better than me would feel bad for her and want to give her a break, but I don't. She brought this on herself. If anything, she'll understand why I'm doing what I'm doing.

I'd bet anything that she'd do whatever it took to bring Greta back if she thought it possible. She can't, just like I can't bring Arabella back, but I can make her pay for what she did.

Night doesn't fall until a few hours later, and by the time the crickets are singing and the stars are out, I'm ready for what I have to do. I ditched my car, not wanting to run into the nosy neighbor with the straw hat again, and I'm dressed all in black.

I look like a cat burglar. If someone were to see me moving around in Amanda's neighborhood, then I'm sure they'd call the cops, which is why I'm going to be incredibly careful. It was easy to park down the road at a gas station and walk to her neighborhood. Now I'm hurrying along the sidewalk, moving quietly, on a mission.

This isn't going to be a long trip. There won't be any looking in windows tonight. Reaching into my pocket, I hold the stone I took from Greta's grave. Of course I took it with me. I have no doubt in my mind that Amanda would have seen it at the grave earlier. She'll immediately recognize it.

She'll know someone was following her.

I feel giddy, like a kid on the way to a birthday party.

When was the last time I was this excited about anything? When was the last time I felt like I was truly alive? It had to have been before Arabella was killed, and it feels better than I'd like to admit to have this glee running through me again.

I arrive at her house. It's locked up for the night, the windows all dark. It feels like every house in the neighborhood is sleeping. Nobody has a front porch light on, and none of the houses I've walked by so far have any lights on in the windows. It's dark and tired; the residents here are completely unaware that I've stopped by for a visit.

Hanging back from the house, I stare at it, drinking in all the details. Since I wasn't able to see into the upstairs, I have no idea which room is Amanda's. I like to think about her in her bed, sleeping soundly, unaware that anything strange is happening outside her window. I love the idea of someone so completely evil being so vulnerable to me right now.

Still, I'm not going to hurt her. The thought of murdering her keeps crossing my mind, but I'm not the type of person to break into her house and kill her. I'm not the type of person to stand over her in her bed and choke the life out of her. I want to see her suffer, but as much as the thought of her being dead thrills me, I don't know if I can do it.

But part of me wants to.

Angry now, mostly at my own ineptitude, I stalk over to her mailbox and pull it open. The small blue rock I took is warm in my hand, and I put it gently inside. For a moment I debate leaving the door cracked so she'll walk over and close it, but then I shut it firmly and lift the flag.

Amanda won't be able to handle the thought that something's wrong with her mailbox, I'm sure of it. I only hate that I won't be around to see the expression on her face when she pulls the rock out of the box and realizes where it came from.

Maybe I could stay. Maybe I could hide out somewhere. I look around me, hoping there might be someplace I can hide, but then I give my head a shake. The last thing I want is to sit here all night long hoping that nobody will catch me, hoping to catch a glimpse of Amanda's face when she finds my gift.

I hate to do it, but I hurriedly walk out of her neighborhood. Nobody moves. No lights come on; no neighbors lean out of their front doors to yell at me to keep it moving. As soon as I get back to my car, I crank the heat and make the drive back across town.

A long shower and a cup of tea should calm me down, but I'm still buzzing on the high of driving Amanda crazy. I dress for bed, knowing I should rest. I have an early morning at the library tomorrow, and if I'm going to keep trying to freak Amanda out, then I need to come up with new ways to do it, but first I text Jackson.

You were right about the letter to the editor. Nothing is going to come of that, but I'm going to take matters into my own hands.

I wait a moment for a response. It's late, and I wouldn't be surprised if he already has his phone turned off for the night. Right as I'm about to silence my phone, it buzzes in my hands.

I know how it feels to do what you need to for the people you love.

I am. That's what I'm doing.
Another buzz.

Be careful. Don't do anything stupid. You want to honor Arabella, but you can't do that from the inside of a prison cell.

I should be happy that he's worried about me and wants me to be careful, but I want him to support me. I want him to see that I'm doing the only thing I can and that nothing can stop me now. My fingers tremble as I type out my response.

I am careful.

Before he can respond, I turn my phone to silent, flip it upside down on my bedside table, and fall into bed, curling up into a tight ball with Henry right at my feet. Of course Jackson is going to tell me to be careful, but that's what he needs to understand — I am.

I'm doing what any person who ever loved and lost someone would do. He can't exact revenge on cancer for killing his wife. If he could, he would. I'm lucky enough to be in a position where I can take revenge on the person who took Arabella from me. Not everyone is as lucky.

Because who wouldn't want revenge on someone who took a loved one from you?

Everyone would. The bigger question, though, is who actually has the guts to do something about it?

Me. I have the guts. That's something a lot of people might not understand, but they will soon.

35

AMANDA

"You're rattled." Dr. Harris crosses her long legs and leans forward to lightly touch me on the knee. "What's going on? Did something happen?"

My laugh sounds forced. "You mean besides someone filing a complaint against me and then writing a letter to the newspaper about me? Oh, and the muddy footprints on my porch and something in my mailbox this morning?"

"What are you talking about?" Dr. Harris's eyes go wide. "What was in your mailbox, a dead animal?" She lowers her voice on the last word, obviously not wanting anyone to overhear what the two of us are talking about.

"No, of course not a dead animal. It was...here." Plunging my hand into the pocket of my white coat, I pull out the blue rock. This morning I didn't have time to stop by the cemetery to see if it was the one I put on Greta's grave, but that's the only thing that makes sense. Someone followed me there, took it from my daughter's grave, and then drove it to my house.

The thought makes me sick.

I hold the rock out, and Dr. Harris takes it, turning it over and over before handing it back.

"A blue rock? Do you think a neighborhood kid stuck it in your mailbox for safekeeping? Kids can be weird sometimes."

"Definitely not a neighborhood kid," I tell her. "It wasn't there when I grabbed my mail last night, and then it was there this morning. Whoever placed it there made sure to put up the flag so I'd check the box and see what was going on." I hesitate, not sure if I can tell her the truth about where the rock came from. It's not that I don't trust her, it's that I don't want to open up that part of my life to someone I only know through work.

"It's a pretty little rock though. Maybe someone wanted you to have it." She smiles at me.

My stomach twists.

"I put it on my daughter's grave yesterday," I say, my voice barely more than a whisper. "Someone must have been following me and put it in my mailbox to freak me out."

"Oh, my God." Dr. Harris takes my hand and squeezes it. "Why in the world would someone do that? From your daughter's grave? That seems wrong."

So wrong. It's so wrong that I can barely think about it. The thought that someone was at Greta's grave after I was, that they know what she means to me, that they would take the rock I left there and then bring it to my house feels like a threat.

But I don't say this to Dr. Harris. I don't want to come across as completely unhinged, not if there's a way to let other people draw the same conclusions that I have.

Someone is out to get me. Someone wants to hurt me for whatever reason. They know where I work, where I live, where I go. They know a lot more about me than I know about them, and that means they're dangerous, whether I want to believe it or not.

We sit in silence for a moment, and I slip the rock back in my pocket, giving it a light pat to make sure it will be safe there. I didn't really think about bringing it to work with me this morning, only knew that I couldn't leave it in the mailbox.

The horror I felt when I opened the box and saw it there...

"Hey, are you okay? You're really pale."

I nod. "I'm fine." It's a lie, and we both know it.

"I think you should call the police. You need to let them know that something's going on. Anyone who knows you and read the letter in the paper would know it's a load of crap, but someone is slandering your name. That's illegal."

She's a ghost in the wind, and that's the main problem. Even if I tell the police exactly what I know about Belle, the fact is that she doesn't exist. She's not on social media. The address she gave the hospital is fake. The number for her doctor doesn't ring through any longer. She's not real, but the person behind her is.

"I have patients to see." I stand up, suddenly needing this conversation to be over with. I like Dr. Harris. Not only do I think she's a kind person, but I admire her professionally. She's the type of doctor who's always willing to go above and beyond to ensure that her patients receive the care they need.

But the way she's looking at me right now makes me want to be sick.

"Okay, Amanda, but you come to me if you need anything, okay? And I really think you need to go to the police about all of this. Whoever is doing this is obviously trying to scare you, and it's working." She stands, clearly waiting for me to respond, so I nod.

"I'll think about it."

But I won't. There's no way I can call the police back to my house, not after they looked at me like I'd lost my mind when

I had them come reassure me the last time. It was clear there wasn't any sign of entry, but I would have sworn that someone was in the house with me, someone was watching me, listening to me breathe.

Dr. Harris is saying something, and I snap back to the present.

"I'm sorry, what was that?"

I hate the look she gives me. Pity. It's written all over her face.

"I said that maybe you need to consider taking a day or two off. Nobody would blame you if you decided you needed a break and wanted to spend some time at home relaxing."

She thinks I'm unable to do my job.

"Or if you decided you needed to talk to someone. Accepting that you need help is hard, Amanda, but if you won't talk to the police, then you might need to talk to someone."

I'm squeezing my hands into tight fists. My nails cut into my palms. All I can do is stare at her.

She really thinks I've lost the plot.

"I'll take that into consideration," I tell her. I've always liked Dr. Harris and I love her friendship but I'm sorry I ever went to her to tell her what was happening. This is something I need to handle on my own, no matter how I feel about her. "Thank you for your advice."

"Amanda —" she begins, but I cut her off.

"We both have patients to see. Have a good morning, Dr. Harris."

I wait until she's gone; then I close the door after her and slump against it. My hand slips into my pocket. A lot of people carry worry stones that they'll rub when they're upset about something or need to calm down. I grip the stone hard, my fingers cramping around it.

I don't care what Dr. Harris thinks. Someone really is trying to hurt me. But who?

We all have people we've wronged in the past, whether on purpose or accidentally.

But whom did I hurt enough to make them torture me like this?

36

COLLETTE

J ackson's face is impossible for me to read right now. I just finished telling him about taking the rock from Greta's grave and putting it in Amanda's mailbox. I wish more than anything that I'd been able to see her face when she found it, but staying away at the great reveal was the only smart move I had.

"You took it from her grave?" There's an undercurrent to his words I haven't heard before. Before I can analyze what he's thinking, it's gone. I wish I could have been recording his voice so I could play it back later to figure out exactly what he was saying.

There was more to his question than the face value of those words, I know it.

"I didn't steal it. I took it to her house and left it in her mailbox. It's not like I took it away and she'll never see it again."

He sighs and runs his hand through his hair but doesn't respond.

"What's the big deal? You're acting like I defaced her grave or something. Jackson, it's a rock. I didn't spray-paint all over the stone. I wouldn't do that."

"Okay." He sighs again. "Okay. I know you're trying to drive her crazy, but what's the endgame here, Collette? You're going to push her closer and closer to the edge until...what?"

I don't want to tell him that I've honestly considered trying to kill her. It's one thing to drive her nuts by following her and looking in her windows and moving things when she's not looking, but murder would make me as terrible a person as she is.

"Who says there's an endgame in this?" I cross my arms, ignoring the cup of coffee I'm holding right now. It's probably cold anyway. Everyone else from grief group is still clustered around the food table, stuffing themselves, but I really wanted to talk to Jackson about this.

If I had known how he'd react, then maybe I wouldn't have told him what I did.

"You can't torture her like this forever. You do know that, right?"

"She killed my sister." My voice shakes. "You don't think she deserves to pay? You don't think she should have to suffer for what she did? She has everything that Arabella will never have, Jackson."

"I know." He puts his hands on my shoulders; it's a gesture designed to help calm me down.

It reminds me so much of how Amanda touched my shoulders when she thought I was coming to her for cancer treatment that I take a step back.

His hands fall between us, then down to his sides.

"It's her," I say. My eyes search his face. "It's her."

"I know." He leans forward. The smell of his cologne washes over me. "I know it is. You know it is. It doesn't seem like anyone else is worried about what kind of person she is, though, does it? You wrote the letter; you filed the complaint; nobody cares."

My head hurts. I take a sip of my cold coffee. Maybe caffeine will help stop the pounding in my skull.

"You're doing all the right things, but if you keep dancing around her, poking at her, she will catch you eventually."

"I know." He's right, no matter how much I hate to admit it. I can keep tormenting her, going out of my way to upset her little by little, but to what end? I'm lucky she doesn't have a security system with outdoor cameras at her house. I'm lucky she didn't see me standing by a tree in the cemetery. How many times have I gotten lucky? And how many more times can I hope that my luck will continue?

"You need to be very careful, Collette. I believe you, but nobody else does. Look at them." He gestures to the group still pigging out on the donuts. You'd think they'd never had circles of fried dough before, the way they're all chowing down. I think how it's perhaps an aftermath reaction to the intensity of grief group. "You really think that Vince would believe you? Linda? Gavin? You think they'd entertain this conversation with you and not be very clear that you've crossed a line?"

He's right. As much as I don't want to admit it, Jackson is right. He's the only one who would believe me. Nobody else here would. I can only imagine how they'd all love to see me locked up for what I've done.

But I can't let that happen.

"What do I do?" I pluck at his sleeve, suddenly feeling like an overwhelmed kid in need of direction from a parent. "I don't know what to do, Jackson."

He opens his mouth to speak, and I lean forward, eager to hear what he's going to say. Jackson is the only person in the world who has any idea how I feel and what I'm going through. He might not have all the answers, but he has more than I do right now, and I need advice.

"You two look way too serious after such a good session." Gavin's booming voice interrupts whatever it was that Jackson was going to say. He throws his arms around the two of us, pulling us close to him. "What in the world could be so important that you need to talk it through over here without the support of the rest of the group?"

"Oh, work stuff," Jackson says, covering for us both.

I look over at him in surprise. Who knew he could lie so easily? I would take a lot longer to come up with an even vaguely feasible alibi, but Gavin seems to have bought it.

"Oh, work," he says, carefully turning us and guiding us back to the group. "Don't I know all about needing to get that stuff off your chest. I'm really glad that you two can support each other, but I don't want you to feel excluded from the rest of the group."

"We don't," I begin, but he shakes his head and laughs.

"Then come on back to the fold, my dears. Let's not let the rest of the evening pass by without you talking to the rest of your friends. I love it when relationships form thanks to grief group, but you need to remember that we're all here to support you."

"There's no relationship," Jackson says, pulling away from Gavin. His cheeks are red, his brow furrowed.

I remember that he's here because he lost his wife.

"Okay, no relationship." Gavin drops his arm from around my shoulder and holds up both hands like he's worried Jackson is going to attack him. "Didn't mean to imply there's something there that really isn't. Friendships are a type of relationship, though, you know. In that way, I think we all have relationships with everyone here, don't you?"

He's deposited the two of us right at the edge of the rest of the group. Like an amoeba consuming a particle of food, they spread apart, making room for us to join them. Linda is telling a story, her eyes bright, her actions animated, but I don't tune in to hear what she's going on about.

It doesn't really matter, does it? The only thing that matters is the conversation I had with Jackson. He's right; I can't keep poking at Amanda and not expect her to hit back. It's true that right now I have the advantage of knowing who she is but her not knowing anything about me.

But how long will that last?

Maybe I was right before. I might not want to admit it to myself, might not want to allow myself to think that it's anything more than a passing thought, but what if getting rid of Amanda is the only way I can ever know peace? I thought I could turn the public against her, could make her lose her job; I thought I could involve the police.

But sometimes, in life, you have to take matters into your own hands. Sometimes you have to be willing to dirty your hands to get what you really want.

Maybe it's for the best that I wasn't able to hear what Jackson thinks I should do. Maybe I need to make up my own mind, listen to myself, give myself the grace and power I need to stand up to evil in this world.

Jackson might have been about to talk me out of doing what I need to. He lost his wife, and yes, that's terrible. But I lost my sister, and I blame myself every single day for what happened to Arabella. Now that I've found her killer, this is my chance to make it right.

It's time to show Amanda what happens to people like her.

37

AMANDA

Tuesday comes faster than I thought it would, marked only by the fact that it's my day to visit Greta. Weekends are a blur of boredom now, as I spend most of my time locked in my house, afraid to go out, afraid to encounter whoever might be following me. During the week, I spend as much time as possible at the hospital, where I'm surrounded by large groups of people. Even though I hate the thought that someone might be out to get me, and I hate that I'm playing right into that fear by allowing it to affect my actions, there's something comforting about being at work with bright lights, lots of chatter, and security guards willing to walk me to my car when I leave work.

Not that anything else strange has happened. Quite the opposite, as a matter of fact. I finally have my car back, haven't seen hide nor hair of Belle Smith, and am starting to convince myself that maybe things aren't as bad as I imagined, when it all comes to a head.

It's misting out, but not enough for me to worry with an umbrella. Picking up the pace, I hurry to the doctors' lot where I parked this morning. I need to go see my baby girl.

After that I can go home, stay in for the night. I'm already thinking about what it will be like to make a cup of tea, maybe even a hot toddy, then curl up with a good book for the evening.

But I stop before I reach my car.

There's a group of people, doctors mostly, but some nurses and patients, all crowded around my vehicle. I can't see my car yet, but I remember where I parked, and I slow down, not really wanting to see what they're all looking at.

"Dr. Morgan?" An ER doctor turns when I walk up behind him. He looks concerned, and I stare at him, still reluctant to look past him to see what's going on with my car.

Until I don't have a choice.

"Oh, my God." Pushing past the man who spoke to me, and shoving my way through the small crowd, I walk right up to my car, hardly able to believe my eyes. My stomach sinks, and I reach out, jerking my hand back at the last minute so I don't have to touch it.

Structurally, my car is fine. Nobody bashed in the windows, nobody ripped off the front bumper. It's in one piece, a smooth matte black, just like it was when I picked it up from the body shop after my accident.

But someone has spray-painted it all over in a garish hot pink. The letters are bold, dripping, so obscene that it feels like someone is screaming at me.

Murderer.

It's written over and over, almost no break between the words so the letters all run together.

MurdererMurdererMurdererMurderer

Over and over. There's no way to catch your breath when

reading it. My eyes flick back and forth across the letters, and they repeat so quickly, without any rest, to the point that I have to close my eyes to stop my own mind from screaming the word at me.

"Dr. Morgan?" There's a hand on my arm. I shake it off.

"I'm fine." It's not the first time I've lied to someone, but it is the first time that I hear the words come out of my mouth, and even I don't believe them. "I'm fine. It's fine. It's going to be fine."

"Dr. Morgan." It's the ER doctor again, and I wish I could come up with his name, but I can't, so when he takes me gently by the shoulder and turns me away from my car so I can look at him instead of the damage, I can't speak. "I'll call the police."

"No." The word is strangled.

He looks at me so strangely, like he can't believe what I said.

"No, don't do that. Let me think about what to do. Let me think about how to handle this."

"I'm sure security has footage," someone else says.

Okay. That's a place to start. I turn, lifting my head, looking for the cameras I know will be present. They have to be here, have to have seen who would do such a terrible thing to me.

There it is. Pointed right at my car. Instead of a shiny black lens, though, it's hot pink, like the paint on my car.

"Someone obscured the camera," I say, pointing. My hand seems to lift up of its own accord. It doesn't feel like my body belongs to me. I wouldn't be surprised if I were to look down and see my body standing there talking to other people while I floated above it.

"Then we definitely need to call the police," the doctor standing next to me assures me. "They'll be able to take care of this, get to the bottom of it."

There's a murmur of assent from the people standing around.

But I shake my head. "Without any camera footage?"

"I'm calling." He ignores the fact that I already said not to and takes out his mobile, walking a short distance away so he can talk undisturbed.

I don't move. I *can't* move. Even though I've been on my feet all day long, I stand still, not leaning on anything, not crouching down to rest my legs.

I just...

It hits me that whoever did this to me could still be watching. *Belle* could still be watching. I turn around, feeling like a fool as I search the parking lot for a hidden figure staring at us.

The only problem is there are a lot of people who are not watching us curiously. I have to slow down, have to look at each individual person in the hopes that they're Belle.

Do I remember what she looks like? Am I confident I'll be able to pick her out in a crowd?

"Okay, the police are on their way." The ER doctor stops in front of me. "Do you want me to stay out here with you until they arrive? I'm happy to wait so you don't feel like you're all on your own."

I manage to shake my head. He looks disappointed, but I can't worry about that right now. The only thing that matters to me is getting out of here. Where in the world will I be safe? Where will I be able to find some peace from this person? Belle, whoever the hell she is, knows I work here. She has to have been the woman in my office, although I don't know why she would do that before we'd even met. She knows what car I drive. She knows where I live, and she knows about Greta.

All I can do is wait for the police to show up and talk to them, but I honestly don't think any good is going to come of this. They couldn't help me when she was at my house; why in the world would I think the police could help me here at my work?

In the end, I don't leave the hospital until three hours later. The police took one look at my car, declared it a hazard, and told me I couldn't drive it. Of course, they had a lot of questions about my past patients and who would go out of their way to vandalize my car like this.

Even when hospital security got involved, I kept telling them that I didn't know. I told them over and over that I had no idea who would do this to me, because honestly? I don't.

Belle Smith isn't real. She doesn't exist.

But the person who wants to hurt me is very, very real.

That's what terrifies me.

38

COLLETTE

I don't tell Jackson about the spray paint. He's been so encouraging, telling me that believing Courtney Barrow is still alive doesn't make me crazy, and now I don't want him to think that I've completely lost it.

"I haven't lost it," I tell myself, tying up my kitchen trash before replacing the bag. "I know exactly what I need to do to get back at her, and I'm doing it. There are a lot of people out there who have no reason to think that she's alive, and that's why they wouldn't understand."

The two empty cans of spray paint are tucked deep in my trash, under some old leftovers I dumped in the bag for good measure. The last thing I wanted to do was throw the cans away in the hospital parking lot trash in case Amanda called the police and they looked for them. I have no idea how easily they could lift my prints, but I have to assume it could happen.

Better to bring the evidence here and dispose of it. It would be my luck that the police in town would actually be good at their jobs for once and they'd be able to put two and two together, realize that I was the one who spray-painted

Amanda's car, and then she'd be able to point her finger at me for everything else I've been doing.

No, it wasn't worth it. But I can't even begin to explain how amazing it felt to spray-paint her car. It was like all of my anger and rage over everything that she's done to me finally got to come out. I was terrified someone was going to see me, but I picked a time when it seemed safe to assume most of the doctors would already be in the hospital.

It was me, the spray paint, and her car. I got to tell her what I really thought of her, and even though I'm sorry I didn't stick around to see how she reacted when she saw my handiwork, it was still worth it. I can enjoy knowing that I'm slowly pushing her over the edge, little by little.

I don't know how else I can drive her crazy without getting caught. Everything I've been doing means I can't go to the hospital or by her house now without risking her seeing me and recognizing me. I know I have to be careful.

This is all for Arabella. If it blows up in my face and I end up going to jail for trying to get revenge for my sister, then I won't ever be able to show Amanda that you can't treat people the way she did. I need to stop her and make sure she never hurts anyone ever again.

That's why, even though I didn't tell Jackson before I spray-painted her car what I was going to do, I pick up the phone. He's going to be at work, so I'm not sure if he'll even pick up, but I mentally cross my fingers while it rings, hoping he's going to answer so I can tell him the next step in my plan.

Enough of this careful tiptoeing around Amanda. I can keep messing with her, and while it does feel good, I want more. The seed of an idea has been growing in me, and even though I'm still somewhat afraid of letting it come to light, it's time.

I want to confront her and tell her that I know what kind

of person she is. I want to look her in the face while she tries to apologize, while she begs for my sympathy.

"Collette, everything okay?" Jackson sounds worried, and I hate that I've done that to him. I don't mean to make him worry about me, but this is the end. I'll confront Amanda, finally feel better about who she is and what she's done, then either go to the police...or handle it myself. In my own way.

"It's fine. Listen, I want you to know that I'm going to talk to Amanda."

"What? No. Why would you do that? Are you sure that's such a good idea?" I don't answer right away, and he continues, "I want to make sure you're going to be safe."

"I am safe." The truth is that I'm so worried I feel like I'm going to throw up, but I'm not admitting that. "She's going to the cemetery after she leaves work. I know she is. I'm going to follow her there, talk to her. I'm going to make sure she knows who I am."

"What's the end goal?"

"To make her apologize. And then she'll admit what she did, go to jail. It's where she deserves to be, Jackson." Barring that...But I don't go there.

"Apologize?" A long exhale. I'm holding my car keys, and they bite into my fingers. "What if she doesn't? What will you do then?"

"I need this to be over." I'm whispering now, not because I'm afraid anyone is going to hear me, but because I'm tired. I'm exhausted by everything that's been going on, and it's time for it to end. He has to see that. He's my friend, and friends want each other to be okay. There's no reason why he wouldn't understand that I'm...exhausted.

"Okay, I understand that. But, Collette, I can't be there this evening. If you wait, I can come. I can make sure everything goes smoothly. I can make sure she doesn't hurt you."

I laugh. "She's not going to hurt me." I picture her trying

to make sense of what's going on. "No, she's going to be so confused. Lost. She's not going to hurt me. I'm going to follow her there, talk to her by Greta's grave. End this."

"Greta?" He sounds confused, but I don't want to go into details right now. I need to hurry to my car, ready myself in position so I can follow her to the cemetery, time it perfectly. The last thing I want right now is to explain everything to Jackson, especially when it's all clear to me.

"I'll let you know how it goes," I tell him, then hang up. He's going to call right back, I'm sure of it, so I turn my phone off before slipping it into my purse.

"Now," I say, turning to pat Henry on the head, "I'm going to end this. Either she apologizes and goes with me to tell the police what she did, or I'm going to kill her."

He meows at me.

"It's for Arabella," I tell him. Tears burn my eyes, and I blink them back, staring at the cat. "You know that, right? This is all for her."

He doesn't answer, but it's not like I expect him to. I follow his gaze across the kitchen.

A knife. Right. If Amanda isn't going to admit what she did and go with me to the police, then I need to be prepared for whatever will come. This has to end, one way or another. I slip the knife into my purse.

This plan will work.

It has to.

It's the only one I have, and if I don't deal with Amanda now, then I'm not sure I'm going to have the patience to give her the opportunity to talk. I don't want to kill her.

But I will.

39

AMANDA

I 'm back in the crappy little rental. After standing there in shock as I watched my car being towed away, Dr. Harris drove me over to the rental place and waited with me until I had keys in my hand.

I know it's the same car thanks to the small cigarette burn right where my head rests. There's nothing nice about this SUV, nothing that makes me feel confident or attractive or successful while driving it, but at least it doesn't proclaim to the entire town that I'm a murderer.

"You're sure you're good to go?" Dr. Harris eyeballs me like she's afraid I'm going to fall to pieces right in front of her.

I could. I honestly could. Everything feels like it's a fever dream, or like I'm watching something terrible happen to someone else, but there's literally nothing I can do to stop it. I want to scream. I want to go to bed and not wake up for a week. I want to drown my sorrows in a bottle of wine.

But all I can do right now is nod. The smile on my face is forced. I feel like I'm like a doll made of hard, molded plastic.

But I don't think she can tell.

On the way over here to drop me off, Dr. Harris was

talking about a hot date she has with her husband tonight. She's ready to go, ready to race home and change, but a sense of duty holds her here until she can be sure I'm not going to fall to pieces without someone watching over me.

"I'm totally fine," I say, waving my hand in the air to brush away her question. "Seriously. I thought I'd avoid patients like this when I didn't go into psych."

She frowns but doesn't answer. "Amanda, I want to make sure you're not going to go home and drink yourself into a coma or anything as soon as I leave."

"I won't." *I might.* "I promise."

"What are you going to do? Do you want to check in with the police?"

"They won't know anything yet. I'll go for a drive, okay? Clear my head. I promise you I'm going to be okay."

"You can call me if you need me." I shake my head, and she sighs. "I'm serious. I have no idea why someone would do that to your car; you're clearly not a murderer. Still, I want you to reach out to me if you feel like you need to talk. I'll answer the phone, okay?"

"Okay, thanks. You're an incredible friend." She is, and I hate lying to her, but there's no way I'm going to call her and interrupt her date. She genuinely is a good friend, though, so it's only a half-lie. "I'm going to be fine. Seriously. I'm not the only doctor in the world who has a crazy patient coming for them."

"True, but you're the only one of those doctors I know and work with." She sighs and finally pulls her keys from her purse. "You heading out now too?"

I wave my keys at her. "Yep. Gonna go for a short drive, like I said. Clear my head. Enjoy some fresh air, and then I'm going to head home, order something delicious to eat, and move on with my day. This could be worse."

"That's what I'm afraid of. Be careful." She moves quickly,

pulling me into a hug that I wasn't expecting, then steps back, holding me at arm's length while she searches my face. "I'll see you tomorrow morning unless you need me before then."

"Tomorrow morning," I confirm. "Have a wonderful date, okay? Don't waste any of your energy thinking about me. I know you have better things to do."

Her laugh fills the air, and she waves once before heading to her car.

I watch her go, my stomach tight, a smile still plastered on my face. I want to be a good friend. The last thing I want is for her to worry too much about me, so it isn't until she finally pulls out of the parking lot that I sag against the rental car.

"Oh, God," I groan, rubbing my temples. "Okay. I've got this. I don't know what in the world is going on, but I've got this."

I'm going to go for a drive, like I told her, but it's not aimless. I'm heading to the cemetery, like I always do. First I stop off at a grocery store to pick up some fresh flowers; then I'm on my way.

It doesn't matter what the weather is like when I'm supposed to go visit Greta. I go no matter what's going on or how dangerous the roads are, and I'm not letting some jerk who vandalized my car stop me from visiting my little girl.

She's gone. I know that. I'm not some distraught, unhinged mother who thinks that her child is still alive and waiting to see her. I know Greta is gone, but I also know that stopping by her grave and taking flowers every single week actually makes me feel closer to her. That's not crazy. That's just remembering my little girl.

The drive is easy. Fast. I'm not surprised that I'm the only car in the parking lot when I pull in. Normally I'd already be here and gone by now, but with everything that went on with my car and the graffiti, I didn't leave the hospital as early as I usually do.

Still, I can make it to her grave, spend some time there, and be back to my car before night falls. There's a quiet voice in the back of my head screaming at me not to walk away from the security of my car when I know that someone has been messing with me, but I'm not leaving my girl alone.

That's one thing about being a mother that a lot of people don't understand. It's not something you can walk away from. Sure, I don't like the way the hair on the back of my neck is prickling, but I need to see Greta. I need to take her flowers.

I'll be fine.

Locking the car, I hold the bunch of flowers close to my chest and hurry up the path to her grave. This is always a walk I've done slowly, enjoying the time I spend by myself while thinking about my daughter, but I'm walking faster than I normally do. The path meanders, and there are gravestones on each side of me.

Once, I think I see something moving behind a large headstone, and I stop. My heart pounds, and I swear my skin suddenly feels too tight for my body. I want to turn and hurry back to my car, but I'm not abandoning Greta.

A large crow takes flight, screeching as it does.

I put my hand on my chest, feeling my heart beat. "God."

A bird, nothing more. Dipping my chin, I hurry on.

The graves back here tend to be forgotten, somewhat neglected, but not my girl's. I cut around a large oak tree and finally walk up to her small grave. I fight back tears at the sight before me.

The flowers from last week are gone.

Whoever was here and took the rock must have gotten rid of the flowers. Why someone would do that to my baby, I don't know. But I do want to know who it is, if it's this Belle Smith who wants to throw me under the bus and get me in trouble at work, but I'm struck again by the fact that I have no way of finding her.

It's one thing to want to hurt me. It's another entirely to bring Greta into it, and I hate whoever has done this to my child.

"Oh, baby," I say, lightly touching the top of her stone. It's still warm from the sun. Moving quickly, I pull the flowers from their wrapping and put them in the vase before realizing there isn't any water in there.

I have to head back to my car, grab my water, and bring it back up. It's already growing darker, shadows deepening as the sun seems to sink faster than it normally does, but what choice do I have? I either bring water or the fresh flowers I've brought for Greta die.

"I'll be right back, honey." My words are loud in the air, and it's only right now that I realize all other sound has stopped.

No birds. No insects singing. It's the perfect time of day for everything to be calling to each other, making their different noises, bedding down.

But there's nothing.

I can't ignore the way the back of my neck feels any longer. Slowly, like that's going to prevent something terrible from happening, I turn around.

There's movement off to the side, and I whip my head in that direction. Panic rises in me, and my hand closes on what I'm holding before I realize what it is and that it won't help me. I force myself to let go, and the plastic wrapping falls to the ground.

"Who's there?" I tell myself I sound brave even though my voice trembles some. "Don't play games, this isn't funny."

Nothing.

Maybe I imagined it. Maybe I'm exhausted and it's all in my head. I take a step away from Greta's grave.

Then another.

One more.

I'm itching to break into a run and put as much distance between myself and the cemetery as possible, but I don't want to look panicked. I don't want whoever is out there to know how upset I am.

One careful step. Then another.

Movement again.

I stop, my heart beating so hard it actually hurts. I'm gasping for breath, trying to stay calm, trying to keep from losing all sense and taking off through the woods like a scared deer, when the shadow I saw steps forward.

Not a shadow, although I already knew that.

A woman. And even though I shouldn't be surprised, even though I knew all along who was behind this, and even though the woman standing in front of me was expected, I feel my shoulders sag.

I knew who was coming. I don't know what she wants.

40

COLLETTE

S he's here. I knew she would be, knew as I raced up the path behind her to Greta's grave. I knew she'd come see her daughter, that it was her day to do that, and that nothing would prevent her from coming by.

What I didn't know was how it would feel to stare at her like this. To be this close to her. Yes, I met her in her office, but we were both lying then. We were using our fake names and pretending like we had no idea who the other person was, but that's all over now. She can't keep hiding from me, and it's time for me to come clean about who I am with her.

The thought makes me giddy.

I stare at her, watching as a host of expressions flits across her face. It's obvious she's trying to decide what to do, how to handle what's coming next. She glances past me, and I know she's thinking about fleeing, but there's no way I'm letting her do that.

I've worked too hard to reach this point, and now I want her to apologize. I want to hear her accept responsibility for what she did. I want her to stop lying about who she really is and finally accept the punishment we both know she deserves. Only then will I feel like I can rest.

This ends here. One way or another.

"Belle Smith." Her voice is flat, her face expressionless. She looks pale, though, like she's not quite sure what's going to happen now that she's called me out. "What do you want with me? What are you doing here?"

"Not Belle Smith," I say, shaking my head. "Collette Jones. Arabella's sister."

Her expression doesn't change.

"You killed her," I say, taking a step closer. "You hit her. You were drunk behind the wheel of a car, and you slammed into her, and then you walked away from the consequences. Instead of facing your trial, you pretended to kill yourself, and now look at you." I wave my arm at her, encompassing the white coat she clearly hasn't taken off after work. "You're masquerading as a *doctor*."

"What are you talking about?" Her mouth hangs open slightly.

"Do your patients know you're a murderer?" I heard her question. I know I need to address it. I can't right now. I need to get this off my chest. "Do they know that you killed my sister and got away with it?"

"I have no idea who you are." She holds out a hand like I'm a wild horse she's trying to keep at bay. "I haven't killed anyone."

She swallows. We stare at each other.

For a moment I hear a whisper of doubt, but then I shake my head. No, I *know* it's her. It has to be her. There's no way it's anyone else; there's no way I could be wrong about this. It's her, and she's keeping up her pretense like she has since she killed Arabella.

But I'm not going to let her fool me the way she's fooled so many other people.

Without taking my eyes off her, I slip my hand into my purse. My knife is there, and it feels good as I wrap my fingers around the handle. I don't pull it out, just hold it, but that small act gives me confidence in my chosen course of action.

"Your real name is Courtney Barrow," I say, taking a step closer to her. "You're a piece of trash, you know that, Courtney? All you do is cause pain everywhere you go. I want you to tell me you're sorry. Apologize, admit what you've done, and I'll take you to the police."

That was the plan. I would make her apologize, and then leave the police to seek justice for Arabella, but now that I say it out loud, now that the words hang in the air between us, I know that won't work. The police failed me before.

My grip tightens on the handle.

"Listen, Collette," she says, now holding up both hands and trying her best to inch her way around me, "I promise you, I don't know what you're talking about. Let's get out of here, maybe grab some coffee, talk things through. Okay?"

"No." I step to the side, blocking her path.

She stops abruptly, lifting her hands higher.

It hits me that she probably thinks I have a gun. Good. Let her think I can blow her to pieces from ten feet away. I don't want her to make any sudden movements or to try to slip past me. Making her afraid of me is the best way to do that.

"I don't know your sister," she says. "I don't know this Courtney person you think I am, either. I promise you, I'm not her. Come with me, and we can talk. I'll prove it to you. I'll show you whatever you need to believe me."

It's tempting, and she knows it is, but I didn't come this far to let her dissuade me from my plan by giving in to a moment of weakness.

"Apologize," I tell her. "On your knees. You are to beg me to forgive you for what you did to Arabella."

She stares at me. Her mouth moves like she's whispering something, but I can't make out what it is.

"Knees! Now!"

She drops like a stone, a whimper escaping her lips.

I'm eager now, eager to move on with this, eager to make her see that she doesn't have a choice in the matter, that I'm the one in control. Carefully I walk closer, not looking down at my feet, refusing to take my eyes off her for even a moment.

She's going to figure out that I don't have a gun. She's going to realize it, and I need to have a plan by then. Sweat breaks out on my brow, but I don't let go of the knife to wipe it away. "Apologize."

She stares up at me. The tip of her tongue darts out, and she licks her lip. She swallows. Her lips move.

"I didn't hear you." I take another step closer. I need to be cautious, need to make sure I don't stand too close to her. She's still dangerous, even on her knees like this. She's a trapped animal, and when creatures think they don't have any way out, that's when you need to be extra careful with them.

"I'm sorry."

"For?" My voice sounds eager, almost excited, even to my ears. "Tell me what you're apologizing for!"

Another step. She still can't reach me. I'm sure of it.

"For..." Her voice fades. She glances over my shoulder, her mouth dropping open. Her eyes widen; her hand flutters to her chest.

I turn to look. As soon as I do, I realize what a terrible mistake I've made. I don't see her move, but I feel her leg sweep against mine. I feel my feet fly out from under me, and I land on my back with a cry.

"No!" Screaming, I pull the knife from my purse, stabbing blindly into the air. I hear her gasp, and a wave of pleasure washes over me.

Did I get her?

I stab again, my eyes squeezed tightly shut; then I force myself to open them and look. She towers over me. Rage is written across her face. I see the way her eyes narrow as she looks at me, how her mouth is a hard line. She shakes her head as I look up and down her body for any sign of blood or injury.

None.

Nothing.

I didn't catch her with the knife. I seriously thought I had, I hoped she would be dripping blood, would be wounded, but I've messed up now.

"What the hell is wrong with you!" She screams the words at me, clearly not expecting a response.

I tighten my grip on my knife as I scramble to my feet.

Rocks and twigs underfoot slide out of the way, and I steady myself, closing my eyes to maintain my equilibrium. For a moment. Then they're open, and I'm staring at her, assessing her. She's a liar. I have to do something. There has to be a weak spot, somewhere I can stab her, can stop her...

I lunge again, my arm out, my knife out, my grip on it so tight I can't possibly drop it.

"You're insane!" she yells as she dances back. "You're crazy."

I need to shut her up. I need to make her stop, make her listen to me. I want an apology, that's all. I want her to go to jail. I need her to see that she can't hurt people and not be punished.

"Why won't you stand still!" No amount of working out could ever prepare me for how I feel right now, how my body is moving. Gasping, I keep coming at her. The air presses down on me; there isn't any sound other than my own breath. When I look at her face, I think she's saying something, but I can't hear it.

My heart pounds in my ears, the thrumming overtaking everything; the hot surge of blood and energy rushes through every part of my body. I close my eyes to absorb the feeling, then open them, ready to lunge. This has to end.

I have to be the one to end it. I have to stop this madness.

I have to stop her.

She's backed up against the headstone, her hands flat on the stone behind her, her eyes locked on me. I can read the name on the stone behind her: Greta.

I take her all in, the expression of fear on her face, the way her feet are spread apart like she's preparing to run. But there's nowhere to go.

I lunge forward, the tip of my knife reaching for her. This is it. Everything I've ever done in my life has been to bring me to this point, to get revenge for Arabella, to stop this woman from hurting anyone else ever again. I feel like I'm flying through the air, following my knife, my entire body stretched out as I aim like an arrow.

My toe catches on a raised root.

I'm no longer flying. Now I'm falling, my knife hurtling free from my hand, my arms out in front of me as I try to catch myself on something, on anything.

The ground flies up at me, and I see a blur of color as Amanda steps out of the way.

The headstone is there, closer, closer. I shut my eyes, seeing the future before it has a chance to happen and knowing full well that there isn't anything I can do to slow time down or stop it.

There's a crunch. I hear it. I feel it. I *am* it.

The pain is exquisite, bright. It's unlike the dull pain I feel when I think about how I lost Arabella. This is so sharp it almost feels cold. It cuts through me, and I want to reach up to my forehead, want to stem the pain, but then I'm on the ground.

She's standing over me. I can see her feet from here. My knife fell, and it's in the dirt right by her. All she'd have to do is bend down. Pick it up.

Finish this. Finish *me.*

She moves. I feel something touch my face, caress my cheek. It's her fingers, warm against my skin. They lightly trace my jaw before she jerks her hand back with a hiss.

"Please," I croak out, but I'm not sure she hears me. I try again. "Please."

41

AMANDA

The first thing I do is fall to my knees and reach out, lightly resting my fingers on the woman's neck.

Belle Smith, but not. Collette, she called herself, but that doesn't help me. I have no idea who she is or what she's talking about. I have no idea who her sister — Arabella, did she say? — might be. My first instinct is to leave her here, let her struggle through what to do when she stands up, but then I stand and take a step back.

Her blood is on my daughter's headstone. There's a knife by my feet, and I kick it away, onto another grave, out of her reach. Even so, I don't think she's going to be reaching for it anytime soon. Her eyes are closed, her temple a bloody mess where she tripped and slammed into the rock.

"I need help," I gasp out. My voice sounds tight. Foreign. Fumbling my phone from my pocket, I dial 911, spinning away from the scene in front of me.

I'm an oncologist. I never wanted to see mutilated bodies in the ER. I never wanted to deal with people who needed to be sewn up because their insides were on the outside.

Covering my mouth, I take a deep breath, mentally preparing myself to speak when someone answers the phone.

"This is 911. What's your emergency?" The woman sounds cool. Collected. She doesn't have blood spattered on her white coat from someone who tried to kill her.

"I'm at Glendale Cemetery. A woman has been following me, and she tried to kill me. She fell and hit her head on the gravestone. I don't...I don't know what to do. She's alive, but I don't know what to do."

"Ma'am, I need you to calm down." Gone is the cool sound in the dispatcher's voice. There's more urgency there now than there was a moment ago, and the change in her tone worries me. "Are you safe right now? And what is your name?"

Oh, God, am I safe?

I turn in a slow circle, looking as critically as I can at everything around me. I don't see anyone hiding in the shadows, don't see any movement. The sun keeps sinking lower, though, and the shadows stretch out farther and farther, lengthening so they look like people.

"I'm Amanda Morgan. And...I think so. I think I'm safe." My voice is a whisper. Even though I don't think anyone is here, I can't help the fact that I'm whispering. I don't want someone to hear me. I crouch down, making sure to keep my back turned to the woman on the ground.

She moans. Fear rips through me, and I turn around to look at her.

"Ma'am, if you're not safe, then I need you to go somewhere safe. Are you near the parking lot? I have units dispatched, and they can meet you there." The urgency is still there. I hate it. I wish she would go back to being cool and collected so I don't have to worry about someone sneaking up behind me, someone ready to kill me.

"I can go to the parking lot," I tell her. Standing up, I look around me once more.

Nothing moves.

The woman moans, her hand twitches, the movement catching my eye, but she's no real danger now. I'm alone with her out here, but I can't stay like this. I'll walk to the parking lot. I can lock myself in my car, wait for the officers to arrive. Then I'll show them where this woman is.

They'll keep me safe. They'll make sure she's locked up so I never have to worry about her coming after me again. I don't know what her problem is, why she thinks I'm someone I'm not, but this has to end.

Even though I'm running to the parking lot, I keep the phone pressed up against my ear. The last thing I want is to accidentally lose my connection with this dispatcher. She's the only person who knows I'm here, the only person who can help me. We're not speaking right now, but that doesn't matter to me.

The only thing that matters is getting help, and she's sending it.

I run into the parking lot, only stopping once I reach my car.

"Come on, keys," I mutter, yanking them from my pocket. It takes me a moment to unlock the door, but then I'm in, my hand shaking as I press the button to lock the doors.

The sound of the system thudding into place allows me to relax.

"Are you safe?"

"Yes. I'm in my car." Even my breathing has slowed down some. I sit in silence for a few minutes, the two of us listening to each other breathe. She gives me updates on where the police are, telling me to hang on a while longer.

She's just told me how close they are when I hear sirens and watch with relief as three police cars pull into the parking lot. They're followed by an ambulance. "The police are here. They're here. Thank you."

"Okay, sit tight for a moment. What car are you in?"

I relay the information to her and watch as officers get out of their cars. The sirens are all off, but the lights are still on, whipping blue and red around the small space. The light reflects off the trees and the little car on the other side of the lot.

Little red car.

I wasn't going crazy after all. Exhaling, I wait until an officer stands right outside my door. I take in his badge, his duty belt. He tilts his head to the radio on his shoulder.

"Okay, Officer Foster is right there with you. I'm going to end this call now, but you're safe, okay?"

"Thank you." My mouth is dry. Carefully I hang up. Put the phone in my pocket. Step out of the car.

Officer Foster towers over me. "Mrs. Morgan?"

"Doctor," I correct automatically, then catch the way he cocks an eyebrow. "Yes. I called 911."

"You said that someone attacked you?"

"Yes. She's up there." I point in the direction of Greta's grave. "She had a knife and came at me. I moved, and she tripped and hit her head on the headstone. She's alive, but it looks bad."

He glances around, and I know he's thinking about how extensive this cemetery is. There's only one parking lot, but the property backs up to a public park and to a residential area. It's sprawling, and without a map or someone leading him to where he's supposed to go, it's likely he'd end up lost.

"I'll show you," I tell him, feeling braver. It's easier to feel brave with an officer right next to me, his gun within reach. Even with the elongating shadows, I'm not worried.

These officers won't let anything happen to me. I'm sure of it.

"I'll walk in front of you; you're right behind me. Tell me where to go, but stay back. I want to keep you safe."

"She's not," I begin. Then stop. "She can't hurt me. She fell, that's what I'm trying to say. She hit her head on a gravestone. She's not going anywhere."

I can't let myself think about how her face looked when she hit Greta's gravestone. The blood had blossomed almost instantly, like a flower blooming, her eyes rapidly unfocusing like she couldn't quite see what was coming for her. It was terrible, disgusting, and I'd stood there and watched it happen.

But now I'm bringing help for her.

My feet feel numb as I follow the officer. He pauses at each diverging path, and I point him in the right direction. We lead a parade of officers and medics, all of us quickly working our way to where I left Collette.

"She's right through there," I tell him, pointing over his left shoulder. He has his gun out, held in front of him, at the ready. No matter how many times I tell him that it won't be necessary, that she can't hurt me now, his training will insist that he's prepared for any eventuality.

Fine. It's probably better that way. The thought of her somehow getting up and coming for me makes me freeze. Then there's a hand on my lower back, propelling me forward.

I walk, but I don't seem to realize I'm moving. Each step feels like one that another person is taking, like I'm watching this peculiar hike in a movie. I keep trying to catch a glimpse of Greta's grave, keep trying to see where Collette might be, but the officer has broad shoulders. He's right in front of me, and I can't see past him.

He stops. I'm so busy craning my neck that I almost slam into him.

"You said she tripped and hit her head?"

There's something in his tone, something in the way he asks that question that should make me pause, but even though a warning bell goes off in the back of my head, I ignore it.

"She fell," I repeat, coming around his side to see what he's looking at. "She was lunging at me with a knife and tripped. She fell and hit her head. I checked her, but she was breathing, she was —"

I stop. He throws his arm out to the side to keep me from walking past him. At the same time, he shifts his weight, effectively blocking me from peering around him.

"I need you to stay where you are." Now his tone has changed. It's lower, deeper, less friendly.

I need to pay attention to him and what he sounds like right now, I know that.

But I can't.

I need to make sure I saw what I thought I did.

"No, she's right there," I say, pushing against his arm. "Let me show you."

He spins like a top, all friendliness gone from his face. "Ma'am, you said she fell and hit her head once. And you were here alone?"

"Yes, I was alone. And yes, she fell. She tripped and fell. Please, what in the world is going on?"

I can hear the sound of fear in my voice. It pitches it higher, and I want to stop, to start over. I need to take a breath, but I realize I can see over the officer's arm, to where Collette fell.

I'm on my tiptoes, straining my neck to see where Collette is. We've stopped a few yards away, but I don't need to be any closer to see her. See the blood. The way her face is caved in.

"I swear, she fell," I begin, but the rest of what I want to say catches in my throat.

She'd had some blood on her forehead, but not much. I'd

been able to make out her features, see the way her eyes unfocused, watch how the blood ran along the side of her nose. Now, though, her face is unrecognizable.

"Oh, my God." I take a step back, bumping into the officer behind me. He steadies me, but it feels like he holds my arms too tight for too long. "What happened to her?"

He doesn't answer. Nobody answers, but I don't really need them to. I see the blood on the gravestone, see the bits of flesh and bone sticking to it. Her face is a mangled mess, blood pooling in the dirt and leaves around where she fell. If I didn't know what the woman looked like before I left her, then I wouldn't be able to tell now.

Her face is gone. There's only a bloody mess in its place.

Officer Foster turns. His expression is cold, steely.

He's talking, but I can't make out what he's saying. I don't have to understand his words, though, to know one thing.

He thinks I did this.

42

JACKSON

Amanda Morgan deserved what happened to her.

It's been six months since she was charged with the murder of Collette Jones, and without any evidence to prove that she's innocent and plenty to put her away, things didn't go too well for the doctor. Of course, a number of people came out of the woodwork in support of her, most of them her patients, some doctors from the hospital, but there are others who stayed silent, who distanced themselves from her.

And then there are others, like me, who are rejoicing that she's finally in prison where she belongs. She pleaded not guilty, but her claims didn't seem to matter to the justice system. She was the last person to see Collette alive. She called the police and brought them right back to her mangled body.

The only thing I regret is that I wasn't able to sit on the jury. But they didn't need me there. The case was open-shut, the way to deal with Amanda obvious to all twelve people charged with deciding her fate.

I'm at my desk, and I reach out, turning the photograph

that sits there, so I can have a better look at my wife. It's from before she was sick, before she lost her hair and so much weight. Lucy was gorgeous, always the life of the party. I remember what it was like to wrap her thick brunette hair around my fist and kiss her, what it was like to pull her towards me into a hug.

I did that when she was first diagnosed with cancer. I promised her I'd stand by her and make sure she got the treatment she needed to survive, and then I did everything I could to make good on my promise. I was there for her through the consultation, the treatment, the long hours in bed when she was so sick she couldn't move.

And all that time, Dr. Morgan promised the two of us that she would make it through. She wanted to try a new experimental drug on Lucy, assuring us that it was the best on the market, that it was going to be a game-changer.

It was a game-changer all right.

Lucy died.

Dr. Morgan deserved to go to prison then, deserved to be locked up so she couldn't ever hurt another person again or enjoy the feeling of freedom while she did so, but she avoided it over and over. Nobody at the hospital thought she'd done anything wrong. It was an *experimental* drug, after all.

But the point was — she used Lucy as her experiment. Dr. Morgan never told us the risks.

She hadn't told us that it might not work, and then it would be too late to try something else. She told us that it was the best option she had for Lucy.

And then she let Lucy die.

A single tear runs down my cheek, and I angrily wipe it away. Grief group was forced on me by my employer, telling me I needed to work through the way I felt, telling me that I had to move past my anger before I could come back to work.

What being angry would stop me from doing at the plant, I don't know, but I did what I was told so I could keep my job.

I went religiously and got cleared to return to work. I did such a good job hiding my rage and grief that I got a promotion. I got a desk job. Everyone thought I was doing great, but they had no idea how angry I still was.

I didn't need to keep going to grief group, but I did anyway. It wasn't that I got anything more out of it, but I knew I was looking for something. Something kept me going week after week, some hope that things would suddenly improve.

And then I met Collette. Poor, delusional Collette, who thought that the person who'd killed her sister was still alive. She wasn't. I looked her up. Courtney Barrow was dead and in the ground, but Collette couldn't come to grips with that. She was a loose cannon, and the only thing you can do with someone like that is point them where you want them to go off and then move out of the way.

And that's exactly what I did.

I pointed her in Amanda's direction. After my wife died, I learned the doctor's schedule. I learned where she went, how much she drank, whom she spent time with. It was imperative that I knew everything about her schedule, and once I knew it all, I only needed to plant the seed in Collette's mind that Amanda was the woman who killed her sister.

It was easy. Too easy. At first, I even thought she was messing with me. It didn't make any sense that she could be so unhinged she would honestly believe that the police wouldn't catch the woman who'd killed Arabella, but that was exactly what she thought. She genuinely thought Courtney was alive, hiding in plain sight, practicing under a false name as an oncologist.

And I took that. I fed on it. Step by careful step, I turned Collette into the weapon that I'd wanted to be.

Then I set her loose on the woman who'd destroyed my life.

Of course, I followed her to the cemetery that fatal day. It was easy enough to park in the adjacent park and make the long haul through the woods to Greta's grave. I'd visited the grave before, wondering why I didn't feel compassion for a woman who had lost her child. But it was all because she had taken my wife from me.

I was there the night Collette died. Neither she nor Amanda ever saw me. Just because the cemetery backed up to public lands didn't mean a lot of people went there. Everyone knew that cutting through the woods took time, was difficult, might result in stumbling into a briar patch.

But I did what I had to. I saw Collette square off against Amanda. I was rooting for her from my vantage point, hoping she was going to do my dirty work for me, but then she fell.

Useless.

I thought for sure Amanda was going to take care of her, give her the help she needed to survive, but she ran off, a phone pressed to her ear. It was then that I knew what I had to do. It wasn't what I wanted. I never expected Collette to die, but the world is not missing out.

Killing her was the only way to give Lucy peace. Now Amanda is going to rot in prison forever, and it's all because of what I did next.

Amanda's voice trailed away down the path as she ran for the safety of the parking lot, and I came out from my hiding place. Collette's eyes were open, unstaring, but she managed to focus on me when I reached out and touched her. My rubber glove made her flinch back, but she couldn't really move. She closed her eyes in pain.

Whispered my name.

I knelt next to her, careful not to leave prints, careful not to snag my pants on anything. The last thing I needed was for the police to figure out that someone else had been here.

"Jackson."

"Collette." I wanted to trace her jaw with my fingertips, allow her to feel some sort of comfort, but there was blood, so much blood.

I didn't want to disturb it.

"Help me." She gasped out the words. It hurt to speak, I could tell, but that didn't mean she wasn't going to try. She was determined to communicate with me. "Help. Me."

"Oh, Collette, I'm so sorry. I want to. You have to know that. But you need to do something for me."

She closed her eyes. Her breathing was labored, but she was still with me. She could still hear me even if she wasn't going to be able to answer again.

"Amanda killed my wife," I whispered. God, it felt good to say the words. I let them hang in the air between the two of us for a moment, waiting to see if she would respond. "I hate her," I said.

Collette's eyes fluttered.

"She killed Lucy. Didn't treat her cancer the way she should have. She needs to suffer, to go to prison for what she did, but she won't. Apparently, it was experimental, no blame attached. You understand, don't you?"

She didn't respond.

"You know what it's like to want revenge for someone you love, I know you do. But I can actually get that revenge. Amanda doesn't deserve to be free. She's a murderer, but she didn't murder the person you thought. She didn't kill Arabella, but she still deserves what's coming to her."

Collette didn't respond. She was close to death, but I couldn't wait around for that to happen. To get what I wanted, to make sure that Amanda spent the rest of her life in prison, I had to make sure there wasn't any doubt. I needed it to be absolutely clear that Collette didn't trip, that she was killed.

"I'm sorry, Collette, that it had to come to this. Thank you."

I forked my fingers through the hair on the back of her head, gripping it into my fist. Collette and I were tangled together, and when I pulled my hand back, her head came with it. I yanked back, then slammed forward, smashing her face into the gravestone.

She never made a sound.

Blood splattered up on the grave, but it wasn't enough. She needed to be dead, not simply injured. I needed to deny her any possibility of survival.

Again I pulled back. Her head was limp in my hand, and I smashed it forward. The crunch was loud, sudden, wet. A squelching sound.

Again.

Bits of meat and bone flew. Her face was obliterated by now, her hair sticking to my skin. Blood flew everywhere, and I finally stood, letting her head fall to the ground. Greta's grave was bloody, the ground a sodden mixture of mud and blood.

No officer who came across this scene would ever think that Collette had accidentally fallen.

Stepping back, I looked around to make sure nobody was watching. The chances of there being someone in the woods keeping an eye on me were slim to none, but, remember, I managed to watch Amanda and Collette, so I knew how to be careful.

But there wasn't anything. Nobody was there to stand as witness to what I did. The police would be here soon, so I backed away, careful not to drip blood, careful not to leave a trail. I had to hurry out of there and make sure nobody would ever be able to point their finger at me. As quickly and cautiously as possible, I picked my way back through the woods.

I smile when I remember how I disappeared into the dense trees, crossed the old rotten bridge over the creek, then took the narrow path back to the park. Nobody saw me come; nobody saw me go.

As I recall the gory events of that night, it's impossible not to feel euphoric about the fact that Dr. Morgan is finally getting what she deserves.

She won't ever be free again. Amanda is where she belongs. Forever. That doesn't bring Lucy back, doesn't negate the fact that my wife died young, in agony, all because of Amanda, but it does make me feel better. Of course, the only thing that would make this all the sweeter would be if Amanda knew the real reason behind her imprisonment.

If I could tell her. If I could look her in the eyes and explain that what she's suffering, and will suffer forever, is punishment for what she did to Lucy. But I can't do that.

Not if I want her to stay where she is. My silence is a small price to pay for locking Dr. Morgan up and throwing away the key.

And as for Collette? Poor thing is finally at peace. She needed peace after her sister Arabella died, and she wasn't ever going to find it while she was still alive.

Killing her was a gift.

Looking down at my hands, I spread them and smile. My fingers have retained the memory. I'm aware of their strength, the power they wield. I can still feel what it was like to palm the back of Collette's head. She was easy to manipulate, easy to kill.

What I did was the only kind thing someone has done for her.

And now that I've done it once, I'd do it again.

THANK YOU FOR READING

Did you enjoy reading *I'm Following You*? Please consider leaving a review on Amazon. Your review will help other readers to discover the novel.

ABOUT THE AUTHOR

Emily Shiner always dreamed of becoming an author but first served her time as a banker and a teacher. After a lifetime of devouring stacks of thrillers, she decided to try her hand at writing them herself. Now she gets to live out her dream of writing novels and sharing her stories with people around the world. She lives in the Appalachian Mountains and loves hiking with her husband, daughter, and their two dogs.

ALSO BY EMILY SHINER

Printed in Great Britain
by Amazon

47330320R00148